HI

ASSASSIN

A gripping crime thriller you won’t want to put down

DAN LATUS

Frank Doy Book 10

JOFFE BOOKS

Joffe Books, London
www.joffebooks.com

First published in Great Britain in 2022

Cover art by Jarmila Takač

ISBN: 978-1-80405-404-8

CHAPTER ONE

Day One

It seemed like an ordinary sort of day when I opened my door that morning and stepped outside to sniff the air and start up the Land Rover. Days like that, nothing happens. You just carry on with ordinary things, and get on with your life.

Or not.

Sometimes I get things wrong.

But it was just as well it seemed to be a quiet day. I had a lot on my mind. Most of it to do with money. In particular, how I was a bit short — and what was I going to do about it? A perennial problem for many of us who are self-employed. Not least a freelance security specialist like me who never knows where the next paying job is coming from . . .

Not eating and walking everywhere looked like the sensible course to take until my boat came in. So this trip to the supermarket in my old Landy looked like being the last time I would be able to afford to do it for a while.

Despite all the nonsense going on in my head as I got moving, some part of my brain was still functioning sensibly behind the scenes. After an automatic glance at the rear-view mirror, I looked again. Then I looked at the wing mirrors and began to wonder.

The black saloon, a low-slung, powerful-looking car, was still there. It was a long way back, but it had been there ever since I had first hit the road, and the distance between us had remained pretty much constant.

Something, or nothing? I didn't know, couldn't tell. But I'd learned long ago not to discount the possibility that something like this might not be an accident, or a coincidence. If it was, fine. Once you've had people hunting you with deadly intent, though, suspicion becomes second nature. Either that, or you're not going to be long for this world.

I had intended visiting the Co-op in nearby Loftus, the biggest settlement in my Cleveland neighbourhood. Suspicion aroused, though, I kept going when I reached Loftus. I kept going all the way into Redcar, another half hour away. I wanted to know if the black car back there was following me, or just enjoying being out on the open road.

The answer became clear as I switched roads and routes, and the space between us stayed the same. I was being followed. No attempt was being made to hide the fact, either. Something was afoot, and even then I felt it didn't bode well.

CHAPTER TWO

I drove into a big and largely empty car park at the Coatham end of the town, parked facing the sea, and waited to see what would happen next. At that point, I was more curious than worried. I just wanted to know what it was all about.

The black saloon, a BMW 7 Series, parked parallel to me, about twenty yards away. Doors opened and two people got out, one on each side, a man and a woman. If there ever had been any doubt about them trailing me, there certainly wasn't now. They wanted something from me. I didn't bother speculating as to what it was. I was going to find out soon enough.

I opened my door, loosened the buttons on the cuffs of my outdoor jacket and slipped the tyre lever I keep handy up my sleeve. I wasn't taking any chances.

By the time I was on my feet and out of the car, the man and the woman had started walking purposefully towards me. I didn't know either of them, and didn't think I'd ever seen them before. I held the car door wide open as a partial potential shield and faced them.

The man looked to be in his late thirties. He had short black hair, neatly combed, and a tanned complexion. The two-piece, lightweight tweed suit and white shirt and dark tie he wore made him look professional, prosperous even. Definitely business class, anyway. But he had a hard face, suggesting his forte was intimidation rather than customer relations or sales.

I didn't take much notice of the woman, who slowed and kept back several paces behind the man. I took in, though, that she looked a few years younger than him, and like him, she was formally dressed. She was small, and wore a dark trouser suit, the kind that I think of as a business suit. Her long brown hair was tied neatly back out of the way in a ponytail, or bunch — or whatever women call it.

'How can I help you?' I called, when the man had halved the distance between us.

He came to a stop. 'Frank Doy?'

I nodded.

'Good. I want some information from you about a couple of people.'

I couldn't place the accent, but he was obviously not from these parts, and probably not even British at all.

'And you are?'

He ignored my query. He just stood and stared hard at me.

'Information, eh?' I said. 'You're going a funny way about getting it. Why have you been following me?'

He ignored that question, too, and asked one of his own. 'Where's Malkovich?'

That was a surprise.

'Malkovich? No idea now,' I said, shaking my head.

'Oh, I think you do. It would be in your interests to give me a better answer than that.'

His arrogance had me bristling, but I curbed my reaction when a pistol appeared in his hand. He studied it for a moment, as if checking it over before using it, making a point.

Then he looked at me again and repeated his question. 'Where's Malkovich?'

'Who are you?' I demanded, concerned now. The gun had appeared awfully quickly in our conversation.

Even the question was worrying. I hadn't expected anything like that. Malky had been gone from my life, and from the area, for quite a few months. My hope was that it was for good. I certainly didn't want any continuing contact with him, and hadn't had any either. Our time together was done.

'It doesn't matter who I am,' the man with the gun said, very deliberately. 'It's what I want that should be your sole concern, that and what I'm prepared to do to get it.

'Let's just say,' he added, 'that I'm in a business not totally dissimilar to your own, and that I'm very successful at what I do. I have a client who has asked me to locate Malkovich, regardless of what it takes. And that's what I intend to do. Given that you're a friend of his, you are where I'm starting.'

This didn't look good at all. The guy was ultra-serious, and I believed him.

I'd also realized by then that the accent I hadn't initially identified was actually some variety of American, and I could guess now what the guy's business was. It looked like I was in serious trouble, for reasons unbeknown to me.

Whatever he thought, though, his business was poles apart from mine, and it seemed now that leading him to a car park as quiet as this one had not been a good idea. It was distinctly possible that I might not leave it alive.

'Do you want to tell me who your client is?' I asked.

He shook his head, just the once.

'Does Malkovich owe money? Has he been tax dodging again?' I asked, trying desperately to spin the conversation out and get some idea of what these people wanted.

He didn't bother replying. He just continued staring at me in a hard, uncompromising way.

'I do know Malkovich. I admit that,' I told him. 'I've known him a long time, but he's not a friend. And I have no idea where he is now. The last I saw of him, a few months ago, he was sailing off in his yacht for good. He had no intention of ever coming back here again. In fact, I had insisted on it.'

I could see that my explanation, true as it was, hadn't cut any ice. The guy looked completely unmoved, bored even.

'Where is he?' he repeated wearily.

'I don't know. We never did do any business together, and had no other reason to stay in touch. That's all I can tell you.'

He sighed and shook his head. Then, with a jerk of his head, he beckoned the woman forward. When she was alongside him, he said to me, 'This is my assistant. She's just learning the business, but she's good, very good.'

I nodded to her. She didn't respond.

'Now you ask him,' he told her.

'Where's Malkovich?' she asked in a flat, equally uncompromising tone.

I spread my hands out in front of me. 'I'm beginning to wish I knew,' I told her.

He handed her the pistol then and said, 'Shoot him in the knee first. If that doesn't work, go on from there.'

Then he began walking back towards their car.

'Get down on the ground,' she told me.

'Come on!' I said, feeling pretty desperate by then. 'It's dirty and wet down there.'

'Just do it.'

I stared at her and shook my head.

'I'll shoot you where you stand if you don't, and that will be worse for you.'

She might well be right. I knew that. But I wasn't going to do it. Fuck that.

'Your choice,' she said, raising the gun.

CHAPTER THREE

The man was ten or fifteen yards away by now. She was less than half that, ten or fifteen feet. I sighed, to signal reluctant acquiescence, shuffled forward a couple of paces and dipped slightly on one leg as if going down. Then I swivelled fast on that leg and swung with the tyre lever that I had allowed to slip down my sleeve and into my hand.

I caught her lower arm, somewhere between wrist and elbow, with all the force I could generate. Bone cracked noisily. She screamed and the gun dropped out of her hand and slithered across the wet tarmac.

I lunged for the gun, but it had fallen behind her and was too far away. Before I could reach it, her partner had another gun levelled at me.

'Back off!' he snapped.

I had to do it. I had no choice. A man will do anything to spin out the last moments of his life — try to make it last a bit longer.

The guy with the gun walked back towards us. 'You hurt?' he demanded of the woman.

Stone-faced, sitting on the ground and clutching her arm, she looked up and nodded. 'He broke my fuckin' arm! It hurts like a bitch.'

So she was transatlantic, as well. Teesside women don't talk like that, in my experience.

The man seemed to consider her answer without taking his eyes off me. I still had the tyre lever in my hand, but I knew I could never reach him with it before bullets from his gun found their mark.

'Well,' he said casually to the woman, 'you're no use to me now, babe. You're just gonna be a passenger, a burden.'

With that, he turned towards her and raised his gun.

That was when she shot him.

CHAPTER FOUR

She had shot him with yet another gun, one that had miraculously appeared in her good hand from somewhere inside her jacket. She shot him three, four times. She just kept shooting until she was satisfied it was done.

He fought desperately to stay on his feet, but he couldn't do it. I swear I heard the life rush out of him just before he collapsed in a heap on the tarmac.

I sensed that the gun would be swinging my way next. Her eyes moved first, her gun hand following close behind. But she had given me the moment I needed, and I managed to move before she had me lined up.

Desperately, I swung the tyre lever again, this time catching the gun rather than her arm. Both went down. I jumped and stamped on the hand that was still holding the gun.

'Leave go of it!' I warned, raising the tyre lever. 'Or I'll break this arm, as well.'

A spasm of pain or anguish crossed her face. Her grip on the gun slackened. It went loose in her hand. She let go. I kicked it aside and stepped back.

'Got any more of these?' I asked, picking the first gun up.

Still sitting on the ground, she shook her head and pulled her jacket loose for me to see. I reached and patted her down as well as I could, without seriously invading her privacy. Then I straightened up and moved around, collecting weapons and studying the bodies — dead and alive. I couldn't help thinking it was a hell of a way to start the day. Not at all ordinary, after all.

'Stay there,' I snapped, as the woman started to get up. 'Right where you are!'

I pointed the tyre lever at her until she slumped back down. Then I turned my attention to the man she had shot. No pulse. Definitely dead. Not a lot of blood, surprisingly. I guessed some of the shots had missed their target. With her good arm out of action, the woman had done well to hit him at all. In fact, she had done well to get the gun out in time in the first place.

Nothing much of a personal nature in the dead man's pockets. A billfold with a hundred quid and a prepaid bank card. A couple of car keys and a stiletto. That was about it, apart from a tissue or two. He'd also had the gun, of course. But, still, he'd travelled light. Professionals in his line of work usually do, and I wasn't in much doubt now about what he'd done for a living. There might be ammunition and possibly more weaponry in the car, but nothing else. Other stuff would be somewhere safe and secret.

What now, I wondered? There were choices to face, and decisions to take, now the action was over and my pulse rate was starting to fall to a more comfortable level. I stared at the woman. Who the hell was she? The guy she'd shot, as well? They were something pretty damned special. That was for sure.

'Want to search me properly, too?' she asked, with a crooked grin.

I shook my head, guessing there would be nothing personal on her either. She was in the same business as her late boss.

'He's dead,' I told her, nodding towards the corpse. 'Very dead.'

'Yeah. Better him than me — or you, for that matter. We're both well out of it.'

Her candour shook me a bit. She was right, of course. It would have been me next, just as soon as he'd done with her. All in a day's work.

'Tough company you keep,' I said. 'Get an arm injury, and you're no further use to him? Some boss!'

She shrugged. 'I expected something. He never liked me.'

'So you came prepared — with an extra gun?'

She shrugged again.

'Well, I can't complain. I owe you.'

'Yeah, you do.' She stared at me and said, 'Your lucky day, Frank. But I wasn't thinking of you when I shot him.'

'No, of course you weren't. He had you in his sights. You had to deal with that first. But you had been going to shoot me yourself, hadn't you?'

'Yeah. A bit at a time, until you told us what we wanted to know.'

Honesty again. There was no accompanying smile to take the edge off. Just sheer, uncompromising statement of fact. I wondered if she really was as hard as she seemed.

'Who sent you?'

She didn't bother replying, and I didn't bother repeating the question.

'Someone who is after Malkovich,' I mused. 'Now who could that be, I wonder?'

A list of possibilities would be a long one. Malky would have made plenty of enemies during his long criminal career. I'd even met a few of them myself, some quite recently.

'You going to let me up?' the woman asked.

Her question brought me up against the more immediate problem I faced. What was I going to do about her, and the situation here? Phone for help? Call the cops?

I looked round to see if there was anyone who might have already done that. It didn't look like it. The enormous car park was pretty well empty. There were a couple of cars in the distance, but no sign of anybody with them. Dog walkers on the beach, probably.

I turned back to the woman. The obvious option was to tell the police what had happened. Get the dead body collected, and her arrested and taken away. That would work.

Yet I held back.

CHAPTER FIVE

Now the action was over, and there was no longer an immediate threat, there were things to think about. If I called the situation in, there would be a police investigation. It would be extensive, intrusive and . . . well, from my point of view, it would probably be of limited value. And it would go on for ever. It might even involve me being arrested and held for a time to assist with enquiries, as DI Bill Peart and his pals would put it. I didn't want any of that.

Most important of all, any such investigation would do nothing to avert another attack on me. I even doubted if it would establish who was responsible for this one, let alone why it had happened.

But what else could I do? Try to get more out of this woman, the hitman's assistant? I was no friend of hers. She would tell me nothing.

Then again, I couldn't just let her go free. Not when she'd come so close to crippling me, and then, probably, finishing me off. There was a lot to think about.

'You could just shoot me,' the woman said, seeming to appreciate my dilemma. 'You have all the guns now.'

'I'm thinking about it,' I told her. 'It would make a lot of sense.'

'It would, but you don't have the guts for it,' she said, with a disdainful sniff that riled me a bit.

She looked away with a grimace then, reminding me — to my satisfaction — that she would be in pain, probably a lot of pain. One arm definitely broken, and the wrist on the other one not much better. Possibly psychologically wounded, as well, after coming so close to being shot by her boss. I ought to be able to use all of that to my advantage.

'Maybe we could make a deal,' she said, looking at me speculatively.

'What? Help each other out?'

She nodded.

'How would that work?'

Seeing that I hadn't just dismissed the idea, she said, 'Like it or not, Frank, we're in it together now. They'll want me now just as much as they want you. Probably even more.'

'Who will?'

She just stared at me.

I stared back, while doing some feverish calculations that told me she might well be right. Laying waste to your boss didn't go down well in any organization, especially one that made a virtue of Old Testament principles.

'Want to see if we can work something out?' she asked.

After only a brief hesitation, I nodded. It might be like sitting down in a nest of vipers, but it could still be worth trying. I needed to know what only she could tell me.

So I swallowed my doubts and made a conciliatory offer. 'On your feet. Let's go and see about getting your arm fixed. Then we'll talk.'

Before we left, the three guns I'd collected went into the BMW. I didn't want them and the cops certainly would when they found the crime scene. No point making life more difficult for them.

My prints being on the guns might make life a little difficult for me, but I would just have to deal with that when the time came — and obviously it would. I was right there, slam-bang centre in this scene. No way could I avoid talking to the cops about it. But I would choose the time to do it.

After that, I took the woman to A & E at the James Cook University Hospital on the edge of Middlesbrough, the main Teesside hospital. We didn't talk much on the way there. She was presumably nursing her pain, physical and mental, while I had in mind that my passenger was someone who had been prepared to maim and, quite possibly, kill me. So small talk didn't come easy.

A right-minded citizen would no doubt have phoned the police and told them where to look for a body and a big abandoned BMW, and also told them what had happened to bring both about. But I have to hold my hand up. I'm afraid that wasn't me. Some passing dog walker would let them know soon enough. But I wasn't going to.

All calls to the cops, anonymous or otherwise, are recorded and traceable. I couldn't afford to be connected to what had happened in a Coatham car park. Not yet, anyway. I needed to know what was happening first, and why. With all due respect to my DI pal, Bill Peart, I believed I would have a better chance of finding that out quickly than Cleveland Police would.

* * *

They dealt with the woman's arm in A & E. It took a while, but it got done. She emerged wearing what they called a splint, with the instruction that she should come back in a few days for them to fit a more durable casing.

'You waited for me,' she said with apparent surprise, when she returned to the reception area.

'Yep. We're going to make a deal, remember? How's the arm feel?'

She glanced down at it, as it rested in the sling, and shrugged. 'It'll mend,' she said, dismissing it.

Probably mend quicker, I couldn't help thinking, with a plaster cast or one of those fibreglass things they tend to use these days than it would in the splint. But what do I know — about any damn thing?

She didn't have her jacket on properly now. It was just draped around her shoulders to accommodate the splint. That meant her other arm was exposed when she moved. She was wearing a short-sleeved blouse, and I noticed that her upper arm was heavily tattooed with some sort of fantasy scene. I wasn't surprised. She was a tough kid. She'd been around.

As we walked back to the Land Rover, I said, 'Your place or mine?'

She looked at me as if I wasn't right in the head and said, 'There's no way in the world we can go back to where I was staying.'

'Someone there will be watching and waiting?'

'What do you think?' she sneered.

'Who was the guy you shot?'

'Somebody important.'

She didn't need to spell it out. I'd got the message. Somebody important. So she had crossed the line and was on borrowed time now. Dead woman walking.

'My place, then.'

She didn't ask where that was. She knew. Probably the people waiting for her also knew. So we couldn't go there, either. And she knew that as well as I did.

I wondered who those people would want most — her or me?

CHAPTER SIX

We needed to talk. I pulled into a lay-by on the Stokesley Road.

'What's the deal?' I asked.

She just looked at me.

'Tell me why I shouldn't just shoot you now.'

She smirked at that. 'You?' she said dismissively. 'Shoot me? Like I said, you haven't the guts. If you had, you wouldn't have let us get to you like we did.'

That riled me again. I have to admit it. But she had a point. Why hadn't I handled it better? I wasn't sure it was lack of guts, though. More like lack of imagination. I just hadn't seen it coming until it was too late to do anything to stop it.

Still, the comment felt like a backward step in our developing relationship. We didn't have to like or respect one another, but mutual hostility wasn't going to get us very far.

I got out and rummaged in the back of the vehicle for a length of rope. Before she realized what was happening, I had looped that around her and tied her securely to the seat back.

She laughed at me scornfully. 'What? You're going to torture me now? You?'

I got back in my own seat and shook my head. 'No,' I said. 'Torture isn't my style, much as you deserve it.'

'What, then?'

'I'm handing you over to the cops, together with a statement about what happened this morning. Friendly cops, I might add. Cops who know me, and have known me a long time.'

She shook her head. 'You can't do that!' she hissed.

'Watch me,' I said, starting the engine.

'OK,' she said, after we'd been travelling in silence for a few minutes. 'Let's talk.'

'What about?'

'You and me — and the goddamn deal!'

I pulled over into the parking area alongside a petrol station and switched off the engine.

'So talk,' I said.

But she didn't. Not immediately. We sat in more silence for a while.

It had started to rain heavily. There was a lot of water on the road. I listened to the swish of passing traffic and occasionally turned on the wipers to clear the windscreen. A big wagon pulled off the road and sent a tidal wave of mud and water over us as it headed for the fuel pumps on the far side of the office building.

I found myself wondering if you could get coffee here. Probably not. If you could, it would be advertised '*Joe's Diner*', or '*Amy's Kitchen*', or something.

'Wet night,' I remarked eventually, giving in, letting her win the undeclared contest.

'How it looks to me,' she said, 'is that you've got more time left than I have. They want information from you, and won't kill you until they have it. Me? They'll shoot me on sight.'

That was honest. It was also something like my own appreciation of the situation. Dead men walking. Both of us. Her first.

'So what's the deal?' I said again.

'It's already started. You've got my arm fixed. In return for that, and helping me get through the next twenty-four hours, I'll tell you why you're in shit street. I'll tell you why we came for you this morning. So you'll know. Then I'll be on my way, and you'll never see me again.'

'That's it?'

She nodded.

She was very sure of herself, I couldn't help thinking. She had it all worked out.

Could I trust her, though? Could I hell!

'What are you going to be doing for the next twenty-four hours, while I'm helping you survive?' I asked.

'Resting. Recuperating. Letting my arm start to fix itself.'

That wouldn't be the whole of it.

'And?'

'And organizing my way out of here. I need to make some phone calls.'

She certainly did. I could understand that. Right now, she had nothing, nothing at all. No passport, or other ID. No money. No bank cards. Not even her guns. Everything she needed was either gone or back in the BMW. Or where she had been staying, the place to which she couldn't return.

I wondered how she would go about replacing the essentials. At the moment, I seemed to be her best hope. Presumably she thought she could do it through me. Was she going to try to sell me the information I needed? Was that the plan?

She guessed the way my thoughts were taking me. 'One thing you can be sure of is you'll have no more trouble from me now. I promise you that. The arrangement where I'm supposed to shoot you is over. I'm through with that.'

'Nice to know. But is it true? Going through with it could help you square things, back wherever it is you've come from.'

She shook her head. 'No way! I crossed the line when I killed their favourite son. In their eyes, I don't exist anymore. They just haven't got round to killing me yet.'

Organized crime, then. It was what I was thinking, and deeply worrying. Even though I still hadn't a clue what it was all about, my chances didn't look much better than the woman's. I needed to find a way out. And there was only one deal waiting on the table for me. We needed each other.

She probably knew that as well as I did myself, and that I would take the deal. Tied up and with only one arm functioning, at least in part, she still held the whip hand. She knew what was going on. She knew things I needed to know, and I knew no one else who could tell me.

I unfastened the rope, threw it in the back and started the engine again. 'You'd better tell me how I can help you,' I suggested. 'Let's get started.'

CHAPTER SEVEN

'Where now?' the woman asked, as I got us moving again.

'Somewhere that is not my house at Risky Point.'

'Good thinking,' she said.

We drove on.

'What do you need, to start getting sorted?' I asked her again.

'A cell phone.'

'That it?'

She nodded.

'Money?'

'I can access money with a phone.'

And everything else, as well, no doubt. Great things, phones.

I wondered who she had in mind to call. Who would provide for her? She might be able to get money herself, but not some of the other things she needed.

'A phone, then.'

'Yeah. Two would be better. That would give me a bit of privacy.'

'Throwaways, presumably?'

She didn't bother replying. The answer was obvious.

'Privacy is difficult,' I told her. 'I can understand why you want it, but I need to be sure you're not just setting me up again with whoever sent you in the first place.'

She frowned, thinking about that.

'You can listen in on the conversation,' she decided.

'OK. I'll do that.'

'Now get me the phones.'

'Yes, sir!'

* * *

I bought a couple of cheap, prepaid phones from an outlet in a small shopping centre in Marton, on the edge of Middlesbrough.

'What about clothes, while we're here?' I asked, after we left the IT store and were passing a clothing shop.

'I'm good. Let's just go. Where to now?'

I'd been thinking about that. We needed phone coverage and we needed to be somewhere where we wouldn't stand out. It would probably also need to be somewhere where deliveries could easily be made by a courier. No point retreating to a cabin in the hills.

I headed for a hotel on the western edge of Middlesbrough, not far from the A19. It was one of those modern places, part of a national chain, that would be frequented by overnighters just passing through. Sales reps, probably, and weary families on their way to or from holidays in Scotland.

I took a room for the night, booked us in and shut the door behind us. Time, now, to talk business and get things sorted.

* * *

'Before I hand over the phones, 'I told her, 'I want to know what's going on. What, and who, made me a target? Let's start with that.'

She sat down on one of the twin beds, her back against the headboard. I sat in the room's only comfortable chair.

'First,' she said, 'you need to understand that I don't know too much myself. My boss picked up the contract off his boss and told me to be ready to go in a couple of hours. I was just his assistant, you understand — his apprentice, he liked to call me.'

'Presumably, this is the boss who was going to shoot you, until you shot him?'

'Yeah.' She paused and gave a wry smile. 'Funny how things work out, isn't it?'

'Very.'

Not really, though. Not to me. It was too damn serious.

I was struck by how little the woman seemed to be affected by what she had done, how lightly she regarded it. No indication of remorse, regret, guilt, or anything else of a sobering nature. More like it had just been another everyday experience.

'It's something to do with Malkovich, is it? Why? What's he done?'

She shrugged and said she didn't know.

'Who's after him?'

'It's no good asking me.'

'I should ask your boss instead? But he's dead!'

So far, this was proving to be a pretty frustrating conversation. I wondered if I should bring in the police, after all. Just hand her and the whole thing over to them. And walk away. Let them deal with it.

As if I could. Already, it was too late for that. We were past the point when I could have done that without being locked up myself.

'I'm supposed to know where Malkovich is, am I?' I pressed. 'Even though I haven't seen him for six months — and before that, hadn't seen him for twenty years?'

'Yeah,' she said.

An answer at last. Something she knew about.

'Even though we're not buddies, or business pals? All because our paths happened to cross a few months ago?'

'You worked with him then, didn't you?'

'I wouldn't say that, exactly,' I said, with a weary sigh. 'Our interests coincided, briefly. Then he sailed off into the sunset on his big, fat yacht — hopefully, never to be seen again.'

'Yeah, well. Like I said, I never knew much about it.'

'But you were going to kneecap me, anyway?'

'Fuck you!' she snarled, eyes flashing. 'I was doing my job.'

''Course you were. As an apprentice hitman.'

She glared at me. If looks could kill . . . ! Let's just say that if they could, I wouldn't be here today.

'Kneecap me,' I carried on, 'and then kill me — a bit at a time.'

'Not necessarily.'

'What, then? Just maim me?'

She said nothing to that. Probably because there wasn't much she could say. She just stared at the wall on the other side of the room as if it was all of no account, which really annoyed me.

'And you were happy to do that?'

'Yes,' she said coldly.

'Pretty damned unreasonable, wasn't it?'

'Not to me, it wasn't,' she fired back. 'No way!'

I stared at her with contempt.

'My life was at stake,' she said. 'I wasn't going to hang back. I didn't know you, and shooting you was going to be my way out of a fix.'

We glared at each other, having got ourselves into a conversational cul-de-sac. I was annoyed with myself now. I'd taken a wrong turning and gone too far. What I wanted was information, not an admission of moral culpability from someone incapable of it.

'Anyway,' she added, calming down before I did, 'it wasn't really about Malkovich. Whoever he is. Not really.'

'Oh?'

'Someone else was the real target, but I don't know who. And that's about all I can tell you.'

CHAPTER EIGHT

'And that's it?' I demanded.

'Yeah. Pretty much.'

It was next to nothing. I mulled over what she had said, without getting anything more out of it. Malkovich wasn't the real target, apparently, but she didn't know who was.

I grimaced, frustrated. This was no good, no good to me at all. Either she really did know nothing more, or getting anything more out of her was going to be a long, slow process. An experienced interrogator was what I needed now.

I got up and wandered over to the window to stare out at the car park. The light was poor this late in the day and it was beginning to rain again. Not much this time. Just drizzle, coming in from the hills. What to do? I thought again about dumping her and leaving her to fend for herself. Once more, I considered contacting the police. I was getting nowhere.

'I need a phone,' she said to my back.

'Probably.'

'At least one phone. You said . . .'

'Use the hotel phone, right there on the bedside table.'

'You know I can't do that. It's a landline. I need a cell phone.'

I turned to face her. 'And I need to know things, a lot of things. I still know damn-all about the attack on me this morning.'

She was about to say something, but stopped when the phone on the bedside table began to make a gurgling sound. We both looked at it. Then I snatched it up.

'Good evening, sir! This is Reception. I thought you might like to know that you have two visitors, who are making their way to your room right now.'

'Thank you.'

I dropped the phone back on its cradle and spun round. 'We have visitors,' I told her. 'They're on their way to our room.'

Looking appalled, she thrust herself upright. 'We have to get out — right now!' she yelled.

CHAPTER NINE

She threw herself off the bed and hurtled towards the door. Then she stopped and turned round to head for the big window. It was one that didn't open, I realized, as she searched desperately for the lock.

Her reaction to the news had galvanized me too. This was no time to stand idly by, wondering what was coming. She knew. And she knew it wasn't something good.

I grabbed a chair. 'Stand back!'

I hurled the chair at the window. It smashed through it and fell into the shrubbery below. Most of the glass went with it. I threw an armful of bedding over the jagged shards left on the sill.

The woman understood what I had in mind. She pulled another chair up to the window, stepped on to it and despite the handicap of having one arm out of action, managed to jump through the gap.

Less adroitly, I clambered out after her and dropped the ten feet to the ground.

We were both up and on our feet smartly. She looked questioningly at me. I pointed to the car park. We set off fast out of the shrubbery, running for the Land Rover. I didn't look back until we reached it. When I did turn, I saw a figure standing in what had been our room, staring out of the hole where a window used to be.

* * *

There was no conversation between us until we were a few miles down the road, heading into the Cleveland hills. As far as I could tell, no one was following us. Why would they? There was no hurry for them. They had all the time in the world.

'You expected that?' I said eventually.

'Something,' she replied, in her usual terse manner.

'Something?'

She nodded.

'You knew they would come?'

'Yeah.'

I didn't doubt it. The only question on my mind was how the hell they had found us so fast. The answer was obvious. They must have been tracking us — her, me or both of us together — somehow.

'Where are we going now?' she demanded.

'I want to find out how they knew where we were. So we're going to see somebody who might be able to help.'

She yawned.

'What? You already know how they did it?'

'I'm tired. That's all.'

'Too bad,' I said with irritation. 'It's all too much for you, is it? Just let me know if you want me to stop and let you out.'

She kept quiet. I kept going, and kept my own counsel thereafter.

* * *

It was very dark, shaping up to be a thoroughly black night, by the time we arrived at Roy Thwaites's garage, even though it was still only early evening. I wasn't surprised to see the garage all lit up. There weren't many hours in the twenty-four when you wouldn't find Roy working.

His '*Star Garage and Auto Repairs*' business was located in Liverton Mine, one of Cleveland's many former ironstone mining villages. The village never had been anything very much, and it wasn't much now either. Just a handful of streets of little brick-built, terraced houses that had lasted an awful lot longer than could ever have been expected when they were put up.

Although it didn't have them now, back in the day it had also had a chapel, a school, and a Co-op store. But that was about it. Still, what more could anyone ever have wanted, back then?

It had been a model village when the mine owner built it, and at the time a good place for working men and their families to live. Far better than wherever they'd lived before, anyway. Now the mine was long gone, and so was the dereliction that had followed its passing. There were just the houses now. And Roy's garage. The latter was based in and around the former mine manager's house, and was the one bit of industry still left in the village.

'How you doing, Frank?' Roy asked, turning away from the car he had up on the hoist.

'Good. You?'

'Can't complain.'

He ran his eyes over the woman and looked back at me with a twinkle in his eye.

'It's not what you think,' I told him.

'It never is, is it? So what do you want this time?'

Roy and I had been pals for a long time, and he knew a lot about what I did for a living. From time to time, he provided services that went well beyond those a garage normally offers. He didn't mind. Perhaps it linked in with the more exciting life he used to lead when he was in the army, in battlefield vehicle recovery. Or perhaps it was just that the money I paid him came in handy.

'I'd like you to run that gizmo you once showed me over the Land Rover, to see if you can find a tracking device.'

He blinked, but only for a moment. 'Like that is it?'

I nodded.

'Time being of the essence?'

'Exactly.'

The woman watched all this, but never said a word. Even when Roy disappeared into the dark cavern where his stores were located, she waited stoically. It was probably because she had no alternative. It certainly wasn't because she trusted me. She wouldn't have done that any more than I trusted her.

Roy returned with an instrument that resembled a wand and began moving around the Land Rover with it.

After making two circuits, he pronounced, 'Nothing there.'

I was very surprised, astonished even. Where to go from here?

Without any preliminaries, Roy ran the gadget around me, not surprisingly without result. Then he turned his attention to the woman and the gadget began bleeping.

'It's her,' he said with satisfaction. 'This thing never lets me down. Sorry, pet,' he added, with a smile.

'So now we know,' I said, looking at her wonderingly.

She just shrugged.

'It will be in her clothes,' Roy said. 'Or her shoes, probably,' he added, glancing down at her feet.

'OK, Roy. Thanks a lot. We'd better get out of here.'

'That you had! And don't let her change her clothes till you're well away from here,' he said with a grin. 'A hundred miles minimum would be good. I don't want anyone coming here looking for her.'

He hesitated and then said, 'You can borrow this, if you like.'

He held out the magic wand and added, 'If it's not in her shoes or her clothes, you really have got a problem.'

CHAPTER TEN

'You OK with that?' I asked as we set off. 'Back to civilization, and a change of clothes?'

'Not much choice.'

That was how I saw it, too.

'If it's not in my things,' she added, 'that guy was right. We really do have a problem.'

I was in full agreement with her on that, as well.

'And I don't do surgery,' I told her.

She rewarded me with a faint smile. Then she turned her head and stared out at the unseeable night-time countryside. I wondered if she was pondering the same thing as me. Had she somehow ingested a bug? Or had one been otherwise inserted in her body?

Being realistic, our deal would be off if the damned thing was part of her. She would be too dangerous for me to be near. Turning herself into the authorities would probably be her best option then, although I doubted very much that she would agree to take it.

I didn't know what my own best option would be if we did split up. No idea at all. But I knew I would be in trouble with the authorities. I wasn't too concerned about officialdom. It was the people coming for me with guns who were the most worrying. I couldn't stop them. I didn't even know who they were, or why I was their target.

All I knew was that besting this woman and her late boss wouldn't be the end of it. These things don't work like that. A contract is a contract, live until it's rescinded — if it ever is. I was no stranger to finding myself in this position, and experience told me it's a hard one to get out of.

'One step at a time,' I said, hoping I sounded positive and confident.

'Yeah. So where are we going now?'

'Back to Middlesbrough, to buy you some new gear.'

* * *

We returned to the small shopping centre in Marton we had used before. When we were there for the phones, I had noticed a women's clothes shop. Nothing special. Just cheap, everyday clothing.

'Here?' my passenger said with a sniff, as I pulled up outside.

'Just get it done,' I told her firmly. 'Find what you need, and then let's get out of here.'

She seemed dubious about even setting foot in such a place.

'Look, whatever you buy here you can throw away once you've got your own money to buy replacements. But right now I'll have to pay, and I'm on a tight budget.'

She said nothing. Just opened the door and got out. There wasn't any doubt about how she felt about shopping somewhere like this, though.

Once inside the shop, she quickly picked up what she wanted. Then I paid with my card, acting the long-suffering male partner.

'Get changed in the back of the Land Rover,' I told her. 'I'll wait outside till you give me a shout.'

I opened the rear door and helped her in. 'Let me know if you need any help. I realize it might be difficult because of your arm.'

The offer of help motivated her to grit her teeth and somehow struggle unaided into the jeans and T-shirt she had selected for herself. Then she climbed back out, and with one hand, slung a denim jacket around her shoulders.

'Good,' I said approvingly. 'You look very different.'

Years younger, I could also have said, and more like the street kid she probably was before she started dressing like a businesswoman.

'That's the idea,' she admitted. 'It might help. Otherwise I wouldn't be ditching a thousand-dollar suit and wearing crap like this.'

That told me! I thought with a grudging smile.

I watched as she pulled on a navy baseball cap and then stooped to put the Velcro fasteners on her new trainers in place.

So. Very different-looking now, but still the same inside. She was still the hitman's apprentice who had been ready to shoot me. I wasn't going to forget that.

'Now the big test,' I announced. 'Come over here.'

We stood behind the vehicle, where no one could see what was going on. I switched on the wand and ran it over her. Nothing. Not one damn cheep. Thank God for that!

I turned to the plastic bag from the shop, which now contained all the clothes she had been wearing, including her underwear and expensive-looking leather shoes.

The magic wand went mad, practically leaping out of my hand with excitement as soon as I showed it the bag.

'So now we know,' she said with satisfaction, and probably with relief. 'It wasn't me.'

I gave her a nod and turned away. We didn't bother spending time locating the bug more precisely. I just dumped the bag and all its contents in a bin on the far side of the car park. Then we got back in the Land Rover.

'Where now?' she demanded.

I almost said we were going to see Henry, but stopped myself just in time. No need to drag him into it. He had enough troubles of his own. He didn't need ours as well. But Henry's world was where we were going.

'Trust me,' I said.

She snorted, letting me know what she thought of that. My feeling was that she didn't, and wouldn't, trust anyone at all — ever. I had no trouble with that. It was exactly how I felt about her.

CHAPTER ELEVEN

I headed for the Railway Hotel in Port Clarence on the north bank of the Tees, immediately opposite where the historic heart of Middlesbrough used to be before it was all pulled down. I wanted somewhere close but out of the way, and offhand I couldn't think of anywhere that better fit the bill. I would never have thought of it myself if it hadn't been for acquaintance with Henry.

Port Clarence, like High Clarence and Haverton Hill, has seen better days. It was built as a model village for the families of workers at the adjacent ironworks and steelworks. The Clarence Ironworks was built by Bell Brothers. It opened in 1854, just a year or two after Bolckow and Vaughan had erected Middlesbrough's first blast furnaces, on the south side of the river. So the north shore has a distinguished industrial pedigree.

That's all long ago now, though. The works, by then owned by Dorman Long, closed early in the twentieth century, and Port Clarence itself began a long process of decline. Now there's not a lot of the place left, and not many inhabitants either. Perhaps a couple of thousand. It's hard to believe many of them have found work, certainly not locally. Dereliction and demolition have seen to that. The remaining houses are kept in decent shape by the relevant authorities, but I imagine you would have to be really desperate, or a native son perhaps, to choose to live there now.

Nowhere in Port Clarence is more forlorn and desperate-looking than the Railway Hotel, which was where I took my passenger.

'Here?' she asked, unimpressed, as I parked in the derelict yard behind the main building, manoeuvring to avoid a corroded oil drum or two and piles of old brickwork from a collapsed wall.

'I wanted somewhere they're not going to think of looking for us.'

'You found it,' she said, with another of her disdainful sniffs.

'It's not as bad as it looks,' I said, grinning as I got out.

Another disparaging snort from within suggested she didn't buy that, but at least she did follow me.

* * *

The Railway Hotel, where once or twice I had met Henry to talk highly confidential and potentially dangerous business unobserved, fitted contemporary Port Clarence perfectly. It, too, would once have been thriving. But now, from the outside at least, it looked derelict and abandoned. Some of the windows were boarded up with sheets of plywood, and there were trees of significant size growing in the gutters. The smoke-blackened brickwork still attested to its origins just outside the gates of the former ironworks.

Unlike the works, though, the hotel had survived. In itself, that had seemed a minor miracle when I first saw the place. Now, as then, the front door was firmly shut and there were no cars parked on the patch of rough ground outside. A handwritten poster on a board in a window offered B & B for the week for £75, as if we were still in the 1950s.

'Nice place,' my companion said, pausing to look around. 'Reminds me of parts of Detroit — the parts that were abandoned when the people fled after automaking moved to the Far East.'

I was astonished by the comment. It seemed uncharacteristically communicative, reflective even. But I just nodded and headed for the door.

I climbed the half dozen well-worn stone steps leading to the front door and tried the handle. It turned, and — somewhat surprisingly if you hadn't been before — the door opened. I stepped inside, into a porch with an ornate tiled floor. Then I went through a second door into a spacious room that could have been labelled either pub bar or hotel lounge. I wasn't sure which term would have been more appropriate.

'Nice fireplace,' the woman murmured, spotting the elaborate white marble edifice that spoke of the hotel's one-time delusions of grandeur.

My eyes were on the only other human being in the place. She was behind the bar as usual, polishing glasses that, so far as I knew, were seldom used.

'Hello, Maggie! How are you doing?'

She peered across the intervening distance and said, 'All right. Where's Henry?'

'Don't know. Haven't seen him for a while.'

'That's all right as well then,' she said, as if my appearance had made her fear the worst.

I walked over towards her, saying, 'We'll have a drink, if you're open?'

'We're always open.'

'And something to eat in a little while, if that's possible?'

'No food. Apart from breakfast.'

I was tempted to ask for an early breakfast, but feared being shown the door for being cheeky. It was that sort of place, and that sort of management.

'I'd like a room for a couple of days, Maggie, if you have any vacancies.'

Behind me, my companion stifled a giggle. Maggie glared at her.

'Don't mind Angela,' I said. 'She has a strange sense of humour.'

'I gathered that.'

Maggie finished drying the glass she was working on and placed it on a shelf. Then she took down a bunch of keys from a hook and said, 'See if any of the rooms on the first floor suit you. Henry usually has number six.'

I thanked her and turned to my companion. 'Shall we?' I said, motioning towards the staircase.

She shrugged and set off, with me close behind.

'Angela!' she said, looking back with contempt as we headed up the stairs.

'Well, I had to call you something.'

'My name's Lady.'

'Of course it is!' I said with a grin.

* * *

I didn't choose Henry's favourite room. I didn't bother even looking in it. The smoke from his cigarettes would be so deeply ingrained in the carpet and wallpaper, never mind the bed, that I couldn't bring myself to believe that even the deepest and most careful cleaning — if that was ever done here — would make any difference.

'Number six?'

I shook my head and carried on down the corridor. 'He's a smoker,' I said over my shoulder. 'A real one, a heavy smoker.'

'I thought smoking was banned indoors in this country?'

'Yes, it is. Legally. But Henry is old school. I don't believe even Maggie could get him to refrain, never mind quit.'

Number ten, at the far end, looked all right when I opened the door. Clean, tidy, fresh smelling, plenty of light from the big window. The double bed had probably seen a lot of action over the years, but you can't have everything.

'This will do fine,' I decided.

My companion walked past me and inspected the room, looking at everything with a critical eye.

'What are you expecting to happen here?' she asked, studying the bed. 'You planning on shagging me?'

'Lady, that's the last thing on my mind!' I assured her.

CHAPTER TWELVE

'So, what do you want?' she asked.

'We have a deal, remember? We're in this together now, you said. So tell me what I need to know, and in return you'll get the phones and any help you need that I'm prepared to give you.'

'Just so's you know,' she said, flopping into the one armchair in the room. 'Anyway, I wouldn't be much good in the sack, with this arm you gave me.'

'You came out of it a damn sight better than I was meant to,' I pointed out.

'Yeah.'

No apology, of course. Not that I expected any. Professional killers are not made that way. It's all about what's in it for them. Sometimes they have redeeming features, but I hadn't seen any yet in this one.

'So let's get started,' I suggested. 'And don't bother telling me again that you know nothing.'

'I'll tell you what I know, but it still ain't much,' she said right back. 'I'm pretty low in the food chain.'

'The fact that your boss was going to redact you because your arm was bust told me that,' I said with a wry smile. 'You were expendable — useful until your capability was reduced. Then . . . goodnight!'

'Ain't that the truth of it?' she said a shade bitterly, making me wonder if her pride had been hurt as well as her arm.

'While you're thinking about what you can tell me,' I said, 'I'm going to let Maggie know we'll take the room. And I'll see if I can get some coffee to bring back with me.'

She nodded. 'You're not worried I'll disappear on you if you leave me alone?'

I shook my head. 'Right now,' I told her, 'you need me even more than I need you. So I'm not worried at all.'

'Got it all figured, haven't you?' she said with a sneer.

'No. Only some of it.'

* * *

Maggie was very helpful. 'Found a room you like?'

'Yes, thanks. Number ten. We'll take that.'

'Good.'

'It's a nice room.'

She nodded. 'Newly decorated. They all are, actually, apart from number six. I've told Henry we'll do that one, as well, if he'll stop his smoking.'

'Fat chance!'

'That's what I think. But you have to try.' She gave a big sigh and added ruefully, 'He's a good man, Henry.'

'The best. We're agreed on that,' I told her. 'But none of us can change his bad habits. Could I get coffee to take back to our room?'

'Yes, of course. That's what this thing is for,' she said, pointing at the shiny espresso machine behind her. 'Not that it gets a lot of use.'

'Business hard?'

She nodded. 'But getting better — slowly.'

'I'm an optimist, as well,' I told her, wringing the first smile I'd ever seen out of that stern face.

* * *

Back in the room, I asked my companion, 'First, what should I call you? You didn't like Angela, did you?'

'Not much, no. It makes me think of nuns.'

'What, then?'

'How about Lady, like I said?'

'If you think that will do?'

'It's my name.'

'Yeah, right,' I said with a smile.

'Really!'

'Oh?'

It didn't matter to me what she wanted to call herself. I picked up the mugs of coffee from the tray I'd brought upstairs with me and handed her one.

'Now we've got that sorted,' I said, 'what else can you tell me? You said Malkovich wasn't really the target?'

'No, he wasn't. It was supposed to be a disguised hit. The person they really wanted to know about was some Russian.'

'Oh?'

'That was the job.'

'A Russian? So how does Malkovich come into it?'

'Georgi, my late boss, wanted to use him to soften you up some. By the time we'd shot you a bit, his thinking was that you wouldn't care what you told us, or who you gave up.'

I just shook my head. These people!

'You're American, I take it?' I said.

'So what?'

'What about your employer — Georgi, did you call him?'

'He wasn't my employer. He was their operative.'

'Their hitman?'

She nodded.

'American, though?'

'I guess.'

It was a bit vague, but I let it go.

'What about the client?'

She shrugged. 'You don't get told that sort of information. I don't, anyway.'

'What do you get told?'

'In my case, which airport to go to, where you're going, nature of target, documents you need.' She drew breath and added, 'Where and when the weapons needed will be handed over. Exit plan. Abort plan.'

I was impressed. Such a strategic approach. I hadn't expected that somehow. She seemed to work for a very professional outfit.

'Nothing personal about target or client?'

'Nothing was said to me. Georgi might have had all that stuff, though.'

Of course. She was there just to pull the trigger, if and when needed. An apprentice. In training.

'It's well organized,' I said, 'but you still have to take a lot on trust.'

'Yeah. You're right.'

'When did you learn I was the initial target?'

'A couple of days ago. When we were driving up from Heathrow. Georgi told me then.'

'You stayed somewhere near where I live? A hotel?'

She shook her head. 'A house that had been rented in advance, where the backup team were.'

A backup team? I hadn't expected that, either. It was beginning to seem like a big operation.

'Where was the house?'

'I don't know. They didn't say. Before you say anything,' she added, 'I can tell you I'm not prepared to go looking for it either. No way!'

Fair enough. She knew what would be waiting there for her. Probably worse than what they'd had in mind for me.

'So, in conclusion, you really were just an assistant, an apprentice? A know-nothing?'

'That's me,' she said with a glower.

We were getting nowhere fast. It was frustrating. But she was all I had, and I didn't want to press her too hard, in case she exploded. I had to play her carefully, if I was not to lose her.

'Come on,' I said, getting to my feet and stretching. 'Let's go and find something to eat.'

CHAPTER THIRTEEN

I asked Maggie for her recommendation on dining.

'There's a chippy just down the road,' she said. 'Nothing else, though.'

'Will it be open?'

'They're open every day, darling. Every evening, as well. A family of workers own it.'

'Chippy?' Lady asked, before I had a chance to find out what Maggie meant.

'Fish-and-chip shop.'

'Oh, I've heard of them.'

'Hungry?'

'A bit.'

'Let's hope it's a good one, then,' I said grimly.

What I didn't say was that thanks to her, I'd had nothing to eat since breakfast and now it was approaching ten at night. Of course, you could say that because of me she'd had nothing either, but I wasn't bothered about her any more than she was bothered about me. We made a fine couple.

I had to wonder if Maggie had picked that up. Probably she had. I didn't suppose much missed her eagle eye and associated antennae. As long as bills were paid and damage avoided, though, it wouldn't bother her. I didn't suppose very much bothered Maggie at all. She was a hotelier, after all.

* * *

The chippy was an oasis, its bright lights reaching out to welcome the citizens of Port Clarence. Many of them were succumbing to its allure, judging by the queue stretching outside the door. Perhaps that was because nothing else was open — or, more likely, even existed.

We joined the back of the queue, which filled the shop and stretched a little way out into the night. I wondered if it wouldn't have been better just to have begged Maggie for some bread and cheese. But the queue moved along pretty briskly, and soon we were inside the shop. I saw then what Maggie had meant about it being run by workers. All the staff looked Chinese, and they were going at it hard. Workers, indeed. I wondered if they were refugees from Hong Kong, come to start a new life where they would be more appreciated.

'This is fun,' Lady said quietly.

I glanced at her, expecting sarcasm and ready to invite her to try to find somewhere else serving food, but I was surprised to see she meant it. She seemed to be genuinely fascinated by the ambience of the place.

'Little Chinatown,' she said, smiling at me.

I nodded. Then I studied the menu on the tiled wall and gave her advice on what to choose. Like me, she settled for cod and chips.

They arrived on the counter, carefully but speedily wrapped in paper after being given a few shakes from salt and vinegar pots. I paid. And we left. Done. Dinner was served.

We didn't go far. We sat on a low brick wall nearby and got started. By then, I didn't much care what was inside the bundle of newspaper. I was ready to eat the whole damn lot regardless.

I have to admit, though, that it was good. Finger-licking good, as I'm sure must have been said by somebody somewhere about such a meal. In America, perhaps?

Lady seemed to think so, too. She didn't say anything, but with her one good arm she got stuck in. Like me, she soon ditched the little plastic knife and fork provided and used her fingers. We made fine progress. Not everything got eaten, I have to admit. But we ate until we were satisfied, and our hunger wrestled back down.

'Ready for a little walk?' I asked, gathering up the wrappings and looking for a bin.

'Sure. Why not? I could do with a bit more air.'

* * *

We walked for twenty minutes or so and then returned to Maggie's hotel. It was pretty busy by then, with two customers sitting on bar stools talking to her.

'All right?' she called. 'Get fixed up?'

'Yes, thanks. The chippy. Perfect.'

'They know what they're doing,' she said, before turning back to her other customers.

We made our way back to room number ten.

'What now?' Lady wanted to know as soon as we were inside.

I'd been thinking about that, thinking about it a lot. I'd had the meal break to put fresh impetus into our discussion, which had been in danger of running into the sand.

'Well, for a start, who's the Russian that somebody is so interested in?'

She shook her head. 'No idea.'

'And why does somebody think they can get to this Russian through me?'

'Pass.'

'It's been a while, quite a long time actually,' I mused, 'since I had any dealings with Russians.'

'Maybe this somebody doesn't know that? So far as they're concerned, you could still be a player in whatever game you were in.'

Maybe. You could certainly explain it that way. There would be some logic to it. Me and what I did with and for the Podolsky family, perhaps. Otherwise, I didn't know what it could be about.

Purely seeking revenge for something else I had done was unlikely. There were always people who wouldn't pass up an opportunity to exact vengeance, but not many would go actively looking for it on such a grand scale. I couldn't think of anyone in that category. The here and now tends to be more important than perceived wrongs in the distant past. What the hell, and who, could be driving this?

Lady, as I was starting to think of her, was very quiet, very thoughtful, now. Very restrained, as well. She wasn't making demands all the time, which was a relief. All the same, I knew I couldn't afford to underestimate her, or her mental and physical capabilities. She was what she was. She could be building up to a maelstrom of violence, hoping to overwhelm me when I had relaxed sufficiently in her company.

On the other hand, of course, she could just be tired and hurting.

'Nothing more you can tell me?' I asked.

She shook her head. 'Not that I can think of right now. As I said, all I really gathered was that Malkovich wasn't their true interest.'

'I got that.'

'It was this Russian woman,' she added with a shrug. 'That's who they really wanted.'

Woman? That brought my head up with a start. She hadn't previously said the Russian was a woman.

'A woman?'

'Yeah.'

'Who, why? What was it about?'

She shook her head. She didn't know. I believed her.

But bells were beginning to chime in my head now. I had a sense of what the possibilities could be, and they were very disturbing.

CHAPTER FOURTEEN

I took the phones out of my pocket and handed them over. 'Here you are.'

Lady looked at me with surprise. 'That means something to you? The Russian woman?'

'Maybe.'

What it meant was that she had given me something, possibly a key piece of the jigsaw even if she didn't know it, and now I wanted to give something back to her. By helping each other, we both might get somewhere eventually.

Still looking at me, she waited for more. I just said, 'Get on with it. Make the call. Do what you have to do.'

'You planning on listening in?'

I nodded. 'I don't want to hear you asking someone for a new gun, not while you're around me.'

She grinned and made her first call. It was a short one. She just recited a bunch of numbers into the phone and then switched off. One call made. It sounded like an automatic check-in procedure, one that she might be required to observe.

With the next one, she spoke in English, to a human being rather than a computer. Again, though, it was pretty brief, and little more than a short list of things she required.

'What do I want?' she demanded with some acerbity when her call was picked up. 'I want a passport, money, a bank card and a clean phone. OK? And I want them now. You got all that?'

I heard a man's voice ask where the delivery should be made. I touched her arm to make her look at me. 'Not here,' I whispered.

She nodded and then paused while she waited for me to suggest somewhere else.

'The steps at the main entrance to Middlesbrough Town Hall,' I said quietly.

She repeated my suggestion to whoever was on the line.

'Two hours?' she repeated, glancing at me.

I nodded.

'OK,' she said into the phone. Then she ended the call, looked up at me and said, 'Done.'

Two hours. That would make it one thirty in the morning. Quiet time. Dead time. Quite possibly literally, if things didn't go well.

I took the phones back from her. She didn't want me to, but, one-armed, she couldn't stop me.

'You might want to use this place again?' she said, squinting at me and obviously thinking of the pick-up venue.

I nodded.

'Or Henry might?'

That made me look at her sharply, wondering what else she knew or had picked up.

'What do you know about Henry, apart from the fact that Maggie and I both know him, and he stays here occasionally?'

'He's the numbers guy, isn't he? Your go-to man for financial information on people and organizations.'

I shook my head. 'He's just a guy, somebody I know.'

'Yeah. Right.'

She yawned, but she had me wondering. She was damn close to the mark. Henry wouldn't thank me for this. He walked on the edge already, always. He didn't need a contract killer knowing about him.

'Here's something I'll give you for free,' she said. 'Henry's days are numbered. He's another dead man walking. They know about him. If he can, he should relocate and disappear.'

'That right?'

She said nothing more. I guessed she wouldn't tell me any more even if she knew any more. But she had confirmed what I had begun to fear. Henry was caught up in this already. Letting me know was her quid pro quo for me allowing her to use a phone, and perhaps for buying her fish and chips, jeans and a denim jacket. We seemed to be establishing the basis for a promising trading relationship.

I was very concerned for Henry, though. He wasn't my responsibility, but I liked the guy and used his services from time to time. Lady was right to think I had a connection with him, but it was as a general research tool rather than as my financial consultant that I knew him. Hell, I didn't even have any finances worth talking about! I certainly didn't need anybody to advise me about them or move them about for me offshore.

I mulled it all over for a while. Then I sent Henry a text, telling him now would be a good time to go off-radar until further notice. And not in his usual refuge with Maggie either. He had drawn the serious attention of unknowns who were looking for both him and me. I added that I couldn't explain it at present, and that I would let him know more when I knew more myself.

'Henry?' Lady asked, after I had sent the text.

I nodded.

'Sensible,' she said. Then she lay down on the bed, twisted around on to her back and closed her eyes.

Ninety minutes to go.

CHAPTER FIFTEEN

Time dragged. I was in two minds about that. On the one hand, I couldn't wait to get rid of this woman who would have maimed and probably killed me if things had worked out for her. On the other, I still believed that whether she realized it or not, she knew things that could help keep me alive, which was all that had stopped me handing her in to the police in the first place.

She said she had told me everything. She knew no more. I didn't believe that. She was part of an organization that held the keys to my future, if indeed I had one. She had to know more than she had told me so far, whether she realized it or not. The question I was struggling with was how to squeeze more out of her. I was hoping that cooperation based on mutual interest would do the trick, but I had my doubts.

I had ninety minutes to do it, to get what I wanted so desperately. Then she would have what she needed. After that, she would probably be gone — if I let that happen, of course.

At the moment, I still controlled all the levers. She couldn't do much without me. On the other hand, there was plenty I could do. I certainly wasn't helpless. One thing I knew for sure was that it wouldn't be in my interests to let her just walk out and disappear.

I just had to hope her supplier didn't provide her with another gun, along with everything else on her request list. That would seriously alter the balance of power between us. I hadn't heard her ask for a replacement weapon, but she lived in a world where guns were standard equipment. There might have been a coded request, or the supplier might use his initiative and include one in the goody bag being sent out to her even if she hadn't asked for one.

I wondered who she had called. Not the outfit she worked for. I was confident of that. Rather than help her, they would want to see her dead, and would probably enjoy making her so.

She had made two calls, both seemingly to people or organizations with whom she was already connected. Family or friends? Unlikely, from what I'd heard. The calls had been conducted on a very professional basis.

I ran again over what I had heard. It was intriguing. The first call had been coded and totally impersonal. Just a recitation of a string of numbers. Nothing intelligible had been spoken, not by her at least. It had just been a way of letting somebody somewhere know she was still in the world of the living.

I doubted if there had been a living person at the other end of that call. Just a machine. It had sounded like her logging in, saying to a computer — and eventually a person — someone, somewhere — *Hi, it's me! Here I am, alive and kicking.* It had sounded just like that.

Then I grimaced as I wondered if the computer could have traced the call and identified our location. Had she thought of that? Did it matter? Impossible to know.

In any case, we wouldn't be staying here more than another . . . what? I glanced at my watch. Sixty minutes now. Fifty-seven, actually.

Whoever she had notified might be able to get a hit squad here in that time, but I doubted it. Where would they be coming from? Nowhere around here.

Anyway, we could improve the odds in our favour by leaving early. We didn't need to stay for another fifty — glance at my watch — fifty-five minutes now.

What about her other phone call? The second one had involved a brief conversation with a human being. That person could have been a friend, but it hadn't sounded like it. She had told someone with the ability to do something about it exactly what she needed, and she had entertained no discussion or argument about it. She expected her demands to be met. Simple as that. And she had felt under no obligation to explain herself, still less to negotiate anything so sordid as price.

So, a commercial business that was part of the professional assassin's supply chain? Very possibly. But she had been so arrogant and peremptory that they could have just turned round and said, '*No deal, baby. Get lost! We don't need your business.*'

People who owed her, then? People she had some sort of hold over. That seemed more likely. *Do this,* she'd said, without allowing for any possibility of them saying no. Either she had something on them, or they wanted something that she had or could do for them very badly indeed. Otherwise, they would have laughed and stayed right where they were when she said *jump through my hoop.*

I wondered how come she had that sort of power, the power to demand and to be served without question. It wasn't what you would expect of an assistant, or apprentice, in any sort of trade or profession. Was contract killing so very different?

Her demand hadn't been a simple one to meet, either. Any organization that could supply what she had asked for at such short notice had a hell of a lot of capability. It wasn't the organization she actually worked for, either. They really would have laughed at her. She had no future at all with them.

I studied her for a moment as she lay there, eyes closed. Who was she? Where had she come from? Nearly everything about her was still a mystery.

She was a tough kid, though. I knew that. Still young, too. But not fresh-faced. Now she was still, I could see that she was tired. Not just weary at the end of a hard day, but bone-tired. The lines on her face told me she had had a hard, wearing life. Probably still in her twenties, and still with some of the prettiness of youth, but her face told me she had been marked by street life. The signs were all there — of poverty, malnutrition and a rackety, unhealthy existence. Little wonder she was a tough kid.

Right now, though, she was tired because it was late at night and it had been a long, hard day. Also, she had pain and reduced capability from the broken arm I had given her. Anyone with an ounce of sympathy would go easy on her, and give her the chance to recover.

But that wasn't me. I'd seen her in a different light, and knew what she was capable of. This was a good time for me to be pressing her hard. I might not get the chance again.

CHAPTER SIXTEEN

Day Two

'Penny for them? Isn't that what you Brits are supposed to say?'

I roused myself and turned away from the window to look at her. She seemed totally relaxed. Despite her broken arm, she hadn't taken or even requested painkillers. Ever the professional, she had kept away from them. She knew what they can do to your response time in an emergency. To me, that meant she was still on duty. I needed to be aware.

'What are you doing with an old English idiom like that?' I asked.

She shrugged. 'Just picked it up, I guess.'

'I guess you did,' I said with a smile.

A moment later, I said, 'Tell me about the guy you shot. Who was he?'

'Someone up-and-coming. Someone important.'

'Who was he?'

'The number one son of the number one boss man.'

Ouch! This made me grimace. It made her situation seem even worse than I had thought.

'That's the boss of the organization you work for?'

She nodded.

'A family organization?'

'You could say that.'

'Mafia?'

She stared at me for a moment before replying. 'Why does everybody assume organized crime is only an Italian thing?'

'Beats me,' I said with a wry grin. 'Too many movies, perhaps? *The Godfather*, *The Sopranos* . . . ?'

'Probably,' she said, with something like disgust at the world's ignorance and prejudice.

Then she closed her eyes again. Conversation over.

* * *

'Time to go,' I said a little later.

'What time is it?'

'One. It'll take us half an hour to get there, check things out and take up position.'

She got up off the bed and sorted out her arm and jacket. I didn't offer to help. I wanted to see how well she could manage on her own. I needed to know what her capability was. But I also had to remember that she could use a gun effectively even with her weaker hand. A broken arm hadn't rendered her a non-combatant.

I wondered if she had managed to get any sleep. I hadn't. I hadn't even tried. No way would I have done with her anywhere near me. I would have been too worried I might never wake up again.

* * *

We left quietly, the world quiet and still, and in darkness. The Railway Hotel wasn't a nightclub. Nor was Port Clarence a lively night spot.

I considered pushing the keys through the letter box for Maggie to find when she opened up in the morning, but opted to keep them for now. It was unlikely that we would be back, but you never knew. You just couldn't tell what was going to happen in the next few hours.

It was cool that night, with a strong breeze coming off the river. Once, the air would have been thick with the products of iron smelting and coke making. The sky would have been ablaze as slag was poured from the furnaces into waiting railway trucks, to be taken away and tipped. The night would have been alive with the screech of machines, the roar of furnaces and the shunting of locomotives. Not now, though. There was nothing now, no sound at all.

'Dead quiet,' Lady said, as we made our way to the Land Rover parked behind the building.

Dead quiet. The utterance had an ominous ring to it.

CHAPTER SEVENTEEN

I opened the passenger door and moved back to give Lady space to climb in. It was as well I did. I sensed rather than saw or heard them coming. There were two of them. Two that I saw, at least.

As I spun round, I saw them coming at me fast. They were a yard or two apart, one slightly in the lead. I heard a click as a knife blade was locked in place, and caught a glimpse of light gleaming on steel.

With a reflex movement, I pulled the door towards me and then hurled it wide open again. It hit the lead guy with a solid thump and stopped him in his tracks.

No time to assess the damage. I moved fast around the back of the vehicle, reached the driver's door and yanked it open. By then, the second man was almost on me. I just had time to grab the tyre lever from the door pocket and swing it round back-handed in a wide arc. It hit. The head or the neck. Somewhere high up. It was hard to tell in the poor light. He gave a grunt and reeled away. I hit him again, hard. He went down, and stayed down.

I raced back to the other side of the Land Rover, just in time to see the first guy falling back from the open doorway, propelled by Lady's two feet thrust into his chest. One swipe with the tyre lever put him out of the fight for good.

Seconds later, I had the Land Rover started and rolling out of the yard. There might have been more than two of them, but I wasn't waiting to find out.

* * *

Even if the Transporter Bridge had been operating at night, it would have been no good to us. We would have been trapped on the gondola while it made its leisurely way across the River Tees. I headed west, through the Clarences, making for Haverton Hill and then the A19. I wanted to get back across the river and into territory I knew better. This side was like the Wild West to me. Besides, we had a meeting to attend at the Town Hall in Middlesbrough.

No vehicle lights followed us. After a couple of minutes, I judged we were on our own, and out of the danger zone. There must have only been the two of them, after all. Perhaps somebody higher up the food chain had thought that was enough to get the job done.

'You OK?' I asked at last.

'I'm fine.'

'It was good you were able to look after yourself.'

'I would have done a lot better if you hadn't busted my arm and taken away my gun.'

I grinned. I couldn't help thinking it was a good thing I'd done both those things. We didn't need more dead bodies trailing behind us.

'How about you?' she asked.

'No problems. We got lucky.'

'Yeah.'

I didn't bother asking who they were or how they could have tracked us to the Railway Hotel in Port Clarence. She wouldn't know that any more than I did.

'What now?' she asked.

'Do you still want to meet the people you called for help — or have we just met them?'

'I need to make the meeting.'

'So it wasn't them, back there at the hotel?'

She shook her head.

* * *

I wasn't too sure about the imminent meeting. In fact, I wasn't too sure about any damn thing. As we sped through Middlesbrough's empty streets, I tried to work through a few of the issues I had in mind. A big one was whether it was sensible to risk the professional killer alongside me picking up another gun from whoever it was she was due to meet? The sensible answer was obvious. I shouldn't let her anywhere near the meeting.

On the other hand, she was still the only person I knew who could help me identify the initiator of the contract on me. That trumped safety-first considerations.

'You don't trust me,' she said flatly, discerning some of my thought processes.

'I didn't say that, did I?'

'No, but it's what you're thinking.'

'You can't blame me for that.'

'What would it take?'

'For what?'

'For you to trust me.'

'Let's just get it done,' I said roughly. 'There's no way in the world I can alter the facts of life. I am what I am, and . . .'

'And so am I?'

'Something like that.'

* * *

'That's the main entrance,' I said, pointing across the street to the main entrance of the enormous old building that once made the Victorians shiver with pride, and that now my mate Henry regarded as a den of iniquity. 'Will they be there?'

'They better be.'

She opened the door and slipped out and away. She was good. After a moment she had simply disappeared into the shadows between the pools of light cast by the few street lights still lit.

I waited and watched until I caught a hint of movement on the steps leading up to the great doors at the front of the building. Then I waited a little longer, part of me wondering if it was a sensible thing to do. If she got what she wanted, I could be back in her sights, the contract still valid. On the other hand, there was nobody else who could help me. So I was reluctant to give her up.

I didn't see her return. It wasn't until fingers drummed lightly on my side window that I even realized she was back. If it had been a gun barrel, not just her fingers on the other side of the glass, I wouldn't have known a thing about it.

I watched her walk round the front of the vehicle. She opened the passenger door and climbed in, awkwardly because of her arm.

'OK?'

She nodded.

'Someone turned up?'

'Yeah.'

'Did you see them?'

She shook her head.

'But you got what you came for?' I said, glancing at the bag she was carrying.

'Most of it.'

'So is this it?' I asked, glancing at her. 'Are you coming with me, or are you going your own way now?'

'I'm coming with you,' she said brusquely.

'Are you sure?'

'We have a deal, Frank. I told you. We need each other. You have to trust me.'

'Mm?'

'Would it help if I told you what I didn't pick up, back there?'

That piqued my curiosity. It was a strange thing to say. 'What might that be?'

'A gun. I didn't take the gun.'

Shit! So there had been a weapon left for her. What a fool I'd been to hope there wouldn't be.

'You didn't take it?'

'I left it right there on the steps. Didn't touch it.'

So her prints were not on it. How very professional, again.

After a moment's further reflection, I said, 'Why? Why did you do that?'

'I thought it might help, with you and me. Will it?'

'What?' I said with a sigh. 'An assistant professional hit-man without a gun?'

'Makes no sense, does it?'

I chuckled and shook my head. But if it really was true, it did help. It helped a lot.

'Come on,' I said, reaching for the ignition. 'Let's go.'

CHAPTER EIGHTEEN

The way they — somebody — had caught up with us at the hotel in Port Clarence was troubling me, troubling me a lot. With no tracker beacon to follow any longer, how had they done it? There was only one way I could see.

'We'd better ditch the phones.'

Lady looked at me. 'You think that's how they got to us?'

I nodded. 'Has to be. We'll get you some new ones.'

Without further discussion, she wound down a window and tossed the phones out on to the road. It wasn't very environmentally friendly, but we had to get rid of them. I couldn't see any other way the people chasing us could have caught up.

'They must have locked on to us when you made those calls,' I said. 'Don't ask me how, though.'

'Did you pay by card at the hotel?' Lady asked, looking for another possible explanation.

I shook my head. 'Cash. I don't think Maggie will do business any other way. I doubt she even has a card terminal. And I used cash at the other one as well.'

'What about at the hospital?'

'I bought a cup of coffee with coins.'

'Buy anything else?'

'Nothing.'

'Had to be the phones, then.'

We drove on, with me keeping a good watch on the rear-view mirror and pondering the question further. What puzzled me was that Lady's phone calls had seemed to be to 'friends' — for want of a better word for them. They couldn't have been to her employer, the people who had an obvious reason to hunt her down.

So were the 'friends' also after her? Not friends of hers, at all? Were they all in it together? Everybody after her?

Perhaps the ambush outside the Railway Hotel had had nothing to do with Lady's phone calls? Perhaps it had been set by somebody else altogether? It could even have been a straightforward attempt at robbery by local villains.

I shook my head. The questions beat me. I had no idea what the answers were. Perhaps time would tell. It usually did.

Meanwhile, there was still something I could usefully do.

* * *

'Where are we going now?' Lady asked after a few minutes, when we had left the town behind.

'To get the vehicle and ourselves checked again. We have to be sure.'

'The same guy?'

I nodded.

'He works night shift as well as day shift?'

'Just about,' I said with a thin smile. 'He's an early starter and a late finisher.'

'Guy like that, he should be a millionaire.'

'One day, maybe.'

But I had my doubts. Roy was good at what he did and he had a good business, but I doubted he would ever make anybody's rich list. He was just a hard-working, capable, decent man, and he had a fine, stable marriage and family life behind him. What more could anyone want? Who needed money as well?

* * *

It was nearly four when we reached Liverton Mine. I didn't know where the time had gone. Very dark, of course. Not even a hint of light in the eastern sky. I didn't expect the garage to be open, and it wasn't. I pulled off the road and stopped a couple of hundred yards away.

'We just gonna waste more time?' Lady demanded grumpily.

'No choice.'

'We got things to do, Frank!'

'They'll have to wait. I need to talk to Roy again before we go any further.'

She wasn't happy, but sensed I couldn't be moved, and settled back in her seat.

'How's the arm?' I asked.

'What arm?'

I smiled to myself. She didn't fool me. I'd seen the spasms of agony cross her face from time to time. She was hurting. All because of what I'd done to her. I could have felt bad about that, but for the memory of what she had been going to do to me.

I got out and rummaged in the back of the vehicle for the rug and the down sleeping bag I kept there for emergencies.

'Try to rest,' I advised, spreading the sleeping bag over her. 'This should keep you warm even if you don't get inside it.'

'And what? We just wait for the guy to wake up and start work?'

'That's about it.'

I got back in my seat and pulled the rug over me. I wouldn't sleep, but if I kept warm, I would at least get some rest. And how I needed that! It had been one hell of a day.

Twenty-four hours, rather, and the twenty-four hours wasn't even up yet.

* * *

The lights went on at the garage at six. They weren't on in the house yet, but the working day had started for Roy. I started the engine and began to roll down the slope towards the lights.

'Get any sleep?' I asked my passenger.

'Not much. You?'

'Like a baby,' I lied.

'Yeah, yeah!'

Roy heard us coming and turned to watch our approach. He stood in the open doorway of the main building, a steaming mug in one hand.

'It must be serious,' he said, when I stopped and got out.

'Morning, Roy! Good to see you at last. I was wondering if you were having a lie-in.'

No smiles. He just took a sip from the mug. He wasn't in the mood for jokes. Too early in the day. Or he didn't like seeing us again.

'You're right, though,' I told him. 'Roy, I want you to run this gizmo of yours over us and the Land Rover again. I might not be doing it right.'

'Same thing?'

I nodded and handed over the magic wand.

'We've changed her ladyship's clothes and shoes, but somebody has still managed to track us. It's driving me nuts.'

I handed over the detector.

'I'll just change the battery first,' he said. 'It might make a difference.'

He turned and disappeared into the depths of his workshop again. By the time he reappeared, Lady had stirred herself and got out of the vehicle. He nodded to her and got to work.

'Nothing,' he said, after completing a circuit of the Land Rover. 'Nothing at all.'

'Us, as well,' I told him, holding out my arms.

Roy ran the wand over each of us and shook his head.

'We ditched our phones,' I told him, 'just in case it was them.'

'They definitely followed you, or tracked you — whoever it was?' Roy asked. 'It couldn't have been a coincidence?'

'Just about impossible,' I told him, shaking my head.

He turned and stared at the Land Rover again.

'Is there some other way?' I asked him.

'Are we talking about one man? A couple of fellows, maybe? Or are we talking about an organization with resources?'

'A big organization,' Lady said, before I could reply. 'One with a whole lot of resources.'

Roy stared at her, impressed by her contribution, or perhaps by her accent. 'Who are you?' he asked.

'This is Lady,' I told him, before she could give anything away, and without appreciating what an opening I was giving him until it was too late.

'Lady, eh?' he said with a smile after a moment or two. 'Do you sing, or are you just royal, an aristocrat?'

'I can sing a bit,' she admitted, with a surprisingly coquettish look. 'Blue-oo moon!' she warbled.

Roy laughed. 'Lady Day!' he said. 'Could that be your name?'

'Ever since I was born,' she said archly. 'How did you know?'

'I know a lot of things. Just ask Frank, here.'

'Come on,' I said, a bit disconcerted by the exchange. What was going on here? This wasn't like Roy. He wasn't a womanizer.

Still chuckling about something that continued to elude me, Roy said, 'My next best guess is that they've got access to the police system for automatic number plate recognition. Either they have somebody on the inside, or they've just hacked into it. I can't think of any other way they could be tracking you.'

'That the Big Brother thing?' Lady asked.

'It is,' Roy assured her. 'Spies everywhere, these days.'

I wondered if he could be right. It was unlikely that the system would have recorded us passing along the road through Port Clarence, but it would definitely have caught us on the A19 and other main roads in and around Middlesbrough.

That would have given them a search area. Not a pinpoint location, but an area to work on. The need to search it systematically would explain why it had taken them a while to find us, or find the Land Rover at least.

That brought me to a decision, and something practical we could do.

'We need another car, Roy. Have you still got that old Volvo?'

He shook his head. 'There's another just like it, though. Do you want to buy or rent?'

'Rent for now. If I total it, I'll buy it off you.'

'Fair enough.'

The usual arrangement. We were well used to it. One way or another, I brought a fair bit of trade into Roy's garage business.

I would be leaving the Land Rover in good hands, confident that by the time I returned to collect it, it would have been given a health check and brought up to the standard required by a battlefield vehicle recovery mechanic.

CHAPTER NINETEEN

'Where now?' Lady demanded once again, as we set off in the battered old Volvo that Roy had assigned to us with the assurance that the motor was good, despite appearances.

'Home.'

'In this crock of . . . ? I just hope we make it. I really do.'

I put my foot down. A storm of muck and rocks blew out behind us.

'All right, all right!' she snapped. 'It's got an engine, like the man said.'

I eased off the throttle, satisfied that Roy had spoken the truth once again.

'By home, you mean your house at Risky Point?'

'That's the one,' I agreed cheerfully. 'Been there, have you?'

'The one place on earth everyone knows about, and everyone will head for?'

'I want to get this sorted.'

'Brother! You've sure picked a hell of a place to do it from,' she said wearily.

It sounded like she regretted being in the same car as me.

'What you're overlooking,' I said, 'is that Risky Point is my home ground. I'm in control there, and in good shape.'

'Let's hope so,' she said with a yawn, making it clear she doubted it.

In the silence that followed, I concentrated on the driving, and considered one of the things she had said. *Everyone.* What did that mean? Who did the term include?

I also wondered if we were up against more than one adversary. There was Lady's erstwhile employer and her 'friend', but was there someone else as well? Someone else who was tracking her? I wouldn't have been surprised, the way things were going.

Then I wondered what this woman was doing, staying with me. She had money and a passport now, presumably. For all I knew, she might also have the gun she said she had left behind. It would have been easy for her to slip into the shadows around Middlesbrough's old Town Hall and disappear. I wondered why she hadn't done that.

One obvious possible reason was that she was still intent on fulfilling the contract she and her boss had picked up. I hadn't ruled that out. Nor had I fully signed up to the idea of a mutual-aid pact. Did she really still need me as much as I needed her?

Taking her back to Risky Point with me was a daft thing to do, in one sense. I tried to keep my personal and business lives separate, even though that often proved impossible. Like now. Yet I felt that if I was to get any more useful information out of her, it would be better to take her back to my place than to another crummy hotel in some other back street of a run-down industrial town. A more friendly thing to do, anyway.

A gamble? Sure. A risk? Yes. But one I still thought worth taking.

* * *

'It's a mistake coming here,' Lady said, as we turned off the road and on to the rough track leading to the two cottages at Risky Point, mine and Jimmy Mack's.

'You think?'

'They know where you live. They'll be expecting you to come here.'

'Maybe. Maybe not.'

She was probably right, of course. But not necessarily. Here might be the last place they would look for me. Why would a man on the run return to the most obvious place in the world for him to go?

Anyway, I didn't much care whether she was right or not. There were practical matters to consider, such as that here was where I held advantages I didn't have anywhere else. Also, I wanted to pull the opposition in close. I wanted to be able to see and feel them, and here was where I was most likely to be able to do that. In short, I wanted to take the initiative instead of just waiting for the next thing to happen and then reacting as best I could.

All seemed normal when we arrived. The cottage was still standing, for one thing. It hadn't been burgled or burned down. No woodsmoke drifted from Jimmy Mack's chimney, but I didn't expect any. He was away from home, convalescing after a hip replacement.

No vehicle had recently crossed the soft area at the end of the track, and there were no vehicles on the gravel patch where I park.

'What now?' her ladyship demanded. It was becoming a question very familiar to me.

'We go inside and get cleaned up. Have something to eat. See if there are any messages for me. Get some rest. Then we'll talk.'

'About?'

'I still want to know what more you can tell me about the folks looking for me. And we need to see if we can help each other further. OK?'

She just opened her door and got out. I sighed with resignation and opened my own door. She wasn't pleased. But, then, I didn't think she was the kind of woman who would very often actually be pleased about any damn thing. She was one hard act.

CHAPTER TWENTY

'Did you build this house yourself?' she asked, as soon as were inside.

'I'm not that old!' I said, shaking my head. 'This place was built over two hundred years ago. I've just tweaked it a bit. That's all.'

Looking around, she said thoughtfully, 'I wondered what it was like inside.'

'You've seen it before, obviously?'

'Only from a distance.'

'You didn't risk peeking through a window?'

She shook her head and continued gazing around at the timbered ceiling and the bare stone walls, as if she liked what she could see. As a proud homeowner, my opinion of her rose a notch.

'You must be feeling pretty grubby?' I suggested. 'You're welcome to take a shower. Or a bath, if that's your preference.'

'I'm OK.'

So much for my offer of hospitality. Perhaps she was worried that bathing would put her at a disadvantage.

I invited her to sit down while I made a couple of mugs of instant coffee.

'It's not your real name, then?' I said, thinking about her exchanges with Roy.

'What?'

'Lady Day. It was a joke, right?'

She shook her head. 'No joke.'

'Oh, come on!'

'My dad was a blues fan, and a club singer, amongst other things. He loved Billie Holiday. And his surname was Day. Work it out for yourself.'

'So your parents really did call you Lady?'

'Yeah. At least, my dad did. I don't know about my mother. I know nothing about her.'

'So it made sense, I guess.'

'I've never had any problems with it.'

'Nor should you,' I said, with a genuine smile. 'Lady Day, eh? It's a lovely name. And it's real.'

She ducked her head in acknowledgement of what was meant as a real compliment.

'So how can I help you?' I asked over my shoulder, as I stirred the coffee. 'Now that you've got money and a passport, and I don't know what else, you could clear off and make your way back home. But you're still here. So what's keeping you? What do you want?'

'Survival.'

I smiled. 'Most of us want that, Lady. So you're still here because you think I can help you survive?'

She nodded.

'How?'

'You're already doing it,' she said briskly. 'I need backup, support and shelter until my arm is fixed.'

'A long job, then. What do I get in return?'

After a long pause, she said, 'I've been thinking about that.'

That sounded promising. I put a mug of coffee for her on the little table near the big armchair where she was sitting.

'Thanks,' she said, surprising me. Then, 'You want to know stuff that you think I know. Right?'

‘Right.’

‘OK. Well, they believe you have something — information about this Russian woman — that they want. Now they want me as well, of course, and I’m here. So they will come here for both of us.’

‘And that helps you how?’

‘The two of us together have a better chance of surviving than either one of us would have on our own. We’re stronger together. Believe me! For it to work, though, I need you to trust me as much as I trust you. Trust. It’s important — believe me about that, as well. That’s why I didn’t pick up the gun that was left for me. I knew you wouldn’t appreciate it if I did.’

What she said made a lot of sense. In fact, such mature judgement seemed remarkable, coming from her.

I still didn’t know, though. I guess I just didn’t trust her that much. How could I?

Yet she was also right about me needing information from her. So I had to keep her here, and keep her engaged. The last thing I wanted was for her to walk out of the door and disappear.

‘You have a broken arm,’ I pointed out, sounding like her late boss. ‘So what use can you be to me?’

‘There are two things you need to know, Frank. One is that you’re right. I do have information that would be of use to you.’

‘At least we’re in agreement about that, then. What’s the other thing?’

‘Broken arm, or not, I can still shoot pretty good. You’ve seen that for yourself. I can shoot to kill, as well. Not many people have that ability, to be able to kill without hesitation. I do.’

It would be no exaggeration to say that she took my breath away. I’d never heard anything like that coming out of anybody’s mouth. Yet I believed her implicitly. She wasn’t bragging or posturing. She was stating a fact.

Before I could respond, she shrugged and added, ‘That’s why people thought I would make a good contract killer, and invested in me. Considering who you're up against, Frank, I reckon you need me.'

I still hadn't got my breath back. Her little diatribe had floored me. I'd never met anyone quite like Lady Day. She was someone who really did know who and what she was, and what she was worth. And she was probably right. I did need her.

* * *

'What else do you want to know?' she asked. 'Let's get to it.'

'Who wants to see me dead? That's my number one priority. Is it the people you work for, or someone else? Then I want to hear more about the Russian woman. I need to try to work out who she is, and why someone has a problem with her.'

Lady took a sip from her coffee mug before saying, 'The first part is easy to answer. I work for 'the brothers', as they're usually called. The Miskov brothers. At least, I did.'

'Until you shot their heir apparent?'

'Only because he was going to shoot me!' she snapped back, bristling.

'I know. I was there. Remember?'

The tension left her as suddenly as it had arrived. 'That's right,' she agreed. 'You were there. You were actually *why* we were there. The brothers had picked up a contract on you, and given it to Georgi to handle.'

'Who issued it?'

'I don't know. That is, I'm not sure.'

'But you have an idea?'

She hesitated before saying, 'It's someone the brothers have been given work from before. Quite a lot of work.'

To slow things down a bit, I studied the floating grounds in my coffee. The water couldn't have been hot enough when I poured it, I decided. Unusual, that, for me. I must have been thinking of something else at the time. I wondered what it could have been. My own mortality, perhaps?

'Coffee all right?' I asked, looking up. 'I can make some more if . . .'

'The coffee's fine.'

'So where are the brothers based? Where do they live?'

'Chicago.'

'That where you're from, as well?'

She shook her head. 'Detroit.'

'But Chicago is your base now?'

She didn't respond. I let it go. It didn't matter.

Chicago seemed a good bet, though, even if it wasn't her home town. It was a city that had always had more than its share of bad guys, and bad things happening.

We sat quietly for a little while. I sensed she was very tired now. We both were. It had been a mad, stressful twenty-four hours. She would be feeling her arm, as well. But it still seemed a good time to press her further.

'They're American, I assume, the brothers?'

She shook her head. 'Russian. Russian-American, at least.'

'Oh?'

But it wasn't too much of a surprise, given that there seemed to be a Russian woman involved in all this.

'What about the initiator of the contract? American?'

'No. Also Russian, like . . .'

She stopped herself, but she knew more. That was obvious. I knew more, as well, now. This was Russian business, without a shadow of doubt.

CHAPTER TWENTY-ONE

So that explained how a Russian woman came into it. Sort of. She was a person of interest to other Russians, who were using a Russian gang to find her. This had nothing to do with Malky Malkovich, or probably the city of Chicago either. Perhaps not even the United States of America. Not really. It was just the traditional Russian way of doing business and settling scores, globally. Think all the way back to Leon Trotsky, killed with an ice pick in Mexico long after he'd left the stage in Moscow.

So they were interested in a Russian woman, one seemingly known to me, and they were prepared to maim and kill me in order to reach her. I wondered who it could be. There were several possibilities, but I was sorely troubled by the thought of one in particular. Sasha. Surely not, though? After all this time?

I hoped desperately it wasn't Sasha they were hunting. If it was, I might well have been dead before Lady and her boss, Georgi, had got anything useful out of me. It wouldn't have been sheer fortitude that had enabled me to hold out. Nothing like that. I simply didn't know anything. I hadn't a clue where she was, or even where she'd been since leaving Risky Point.

I thought ruefully of the last conversation I'd had with Sasha, a defecting Russian intelligence agent I had been quite close to at one time, and how she had said she wouldn't tell me where she was going to start her new life. She wouldn't tell me, she said, because one day someone would arrive who wanted to know where she was, and it would be better for us both if I didn't know.

Better for Sasha, I thought with a wry smile — and I didn't begrudge her that — but not so good for me. Still, she was right. Under duress, everybody talks eventually. The optimists and philosophers who claim torture never works simply deny the historical evidence. The Gestapo and the NKVD were not the only organizations that had found it worked just fine for them.

* * *

'Who did you call for help?' I asked Lady.

'You don't need to know, Frank,' she said briskly. 'That's my business.'

'I don't need to know a lot of things,' I countered, 'but this, I do. Someone responded remarkably readily to your call, someone with a lot of clout, who is on your side. I know it wasn't the Miskov brothers. So who was it? We may need them again.'

'I called a friend.'

'Must be a very good friend!'

She just played a dead bat to that one and said nothing. I let it go for now. She wasn't going to say anything more. Not now. Not intentionally, anyway. I could wait.

One thing I was sure of — it hadn't been a friend of the normal kind. The conversation had been terse, very limited and devoid of emotion. There had been no desperate appeal for help. She had just listed her requirements as if she had no doubt at all that her demands would be fully met, and the person at the other end had simply taken the order and delivered. No bargaining had been required. No price had been mentioned.

Someone, somewhere, wanted her to have whatever she needed, and wasn't about to question or deny her. Yet what sort of 'friend' was capable of producing a new passport at such short notice?

* * *

'Who will the Brotherhood send after you? Do you know?'

She hesitated. 'Well, Georgi's backup team, led by Lucas, will be first in line. They are already here. Maybe someone else, as well. I don't know.'

'Will they come here?'

'Probably.'

'Soon?'

'Maybe not. There's Georgi to be dealt with first.'

'You've already done that. He's dead. Remember?'

'Yes, but the brothers will want to get him home and give him due ceremony. I don't know how they'll deal with that. Maybe Lucas, maybe a lawyer. I just don't know,' she finished with a shrug.

'So we have a little time?'

She didn't respond.

'If the brothers will need time to get organized, who has been chasing us? Lucas and the backup team?'

'Probably. They must have learned what happened and come looking for me. But they're nothing special,' she added dismissively.

Even so, I thought, special or not, they had found us very quickly at the first hotel, and then again in Port Clarence. We'd have to be ready for them to come for us at Risky Point, too.

'They're not who I'm really worried about,' she added.

'Who then?'

'The brothers have a clean-up guy on staff. Zimmerman.'

'Another hitman?'

'They call him the Auditor. They use him for internal disciplinary purposes.'

I could imagine what his work entailed!

'You think they'll send him after you?'

After a brief hesitation, she said, 'Maybe. He doesn't like me. He's deeply prejudiced.'

'About what?'

She stopped herself saying what she was thinking, but only just. I wondered what it was.

CHAPTER TWENTY-TWO

The day was cracking on. Late morning now. Soon be noon. And we had a problem. We were both knackered, totally exhausted. Responding to crisis after crisis over the last twenty-four-plus hours had taken its toll, physically and psychologically. I knew I needed to get some sleep, if I wasn't going to collapse in a heap. I didn't suppose Lady would be much different, even if she was a few years younger than me. If anything, she looked as if she was in a worse state than me.

We could have taken turns, one sleeping while the other kept watch, but I wasn't going to suggest that. Partly, it was because I didn't feel confident that whoever took first watch would stay awake for several hours while the other one slept. It was also because I just didn't trust Lady well enough, despite our agreement. It was too soon. I wasn't too concerned about the possibility of a knife in the ribs while I was unconscious, but how could I know what might happen if an emissary from the Miskov brothers arrived while I was asleep?

Fortunately, there was a simple way of coping with all these issues. We wouldn't stay here. There was no need. We would go somewhere safer.

'We both need to get some rest,' I said, 'but we're not going to do it here. Come on! We're moving.'

'So soon?' Lady said, sounding disappointed.

'Yep. We're going to a safer place to do it.'

* * *

I stuffed a few things we needed in a rucksack and checked to make sure the CCTV was working. Then I pulled a couple of heavy-duty outdoor jackets off their pegs and tossed one to Lady.

'We'll need them,' I told her.

'Why?'

'To stop us getting cold and wet. OK? That's it. We're ready. Let's go!'

Looking thoroughly disenchanted, Lady scowled and followed me out of the door.

'Where now?' she demanded.

'You need to trust me,' I said with a grin. 'Remember?'

I led the way past Jimmy Mack's cottage, thankful that he wasn't in residence at present, and over to the edge of the cliff. Lady hung back.

'It's all right,' I assured her. 'We're walking down to the beach. We're not jumping.'

When she still looked reluctant to follow me, I added, 'Don't worry so much. We'll have a roof over our heads. We're not going to be out in the open.'

That assurance tipped the scales. She moved forward hesitantly. Belatedly, I realized something I should have thought of earlier. She was a city girl. She just didn't trust the Great Outdoors.

Although it may look pretty terrifying if you're not used to it, there is a rough route down the cliff face. Very rough. I hesitate to call it a path. It's just a way that's been used for time immemorial by fishermen, and latterly by me and Jimmy Mack when we want to reach his Whitby coble. The boat is kept on the little shingle beach at the foot of the cliff, a small patch above the high-water mark that usually stays dry. The haven is an unusual feature on this coast, and probably explains why our two cottages exist. Jimmy certainly isn't the first fisherman to have taken advantage of it.

The shale and mudstone this cliff is largely made of becomes extremely greasy and slippery when wet, which is much of the time apart from in midsummer, and often enough even then. The route is particularly hazardous in poor light. You have to know where you're going.

A while ago, partly in response to Jimmy Mack's growing arthritis problem, I had installed a heavy-duty hemp rope alongside what we actually do call the 'path', even if really it isn't one. The rope is something to hang on to for balance and safety on the descent and something to haul yourself up by on the climb. Without it, I doubt Jimmy would be able to get down to the beach at all these days, and I have to admit it makes things easier for me, too.

'Hold on to the rope with your good hand,' I advised Lady, 'and don't look down. Just stick close to me, and you'll be all right.'

'Get on with it,' she snapped.

I smiled to myself. It was good to know something could unsettle her. In a way, it was a comfort to know I had her at a disadvantage. I would just have to watch out that she didn't change her mind about our alliance and give me a push in the back. Nobody survived a fall from this cliff.

The descent was a bit of a challenge for her, but she managed. We got down to the bottom in one piece.

'That where we're going?' she asked, looking at the cabin tucked up against the base of the cliff.

'That's it. Home from home!'

It was no more than a very simple, one-room shed, but it wasn't a bad little refuge from cold, wind, rain, sleet and anything else Mother Nature chose to throw. With a couple of bunk beds against one wall, a wood-burning stove for driftwood from the beach and a couple of easy chairs, it made a very snug little retreat.

'Sit down!' I invited my guest when we got inside. 'I'll make you a cup of coffee.'

'How?' she demanded.

I pulled a little gas camping stove out of a cupboard and placed it on the kitchen table that dominated the floor space.

She looked askance at it for a moment and then decided to cheer up. 'OK,' she said, 'but you'll need water, as well. And sea water won't be any good.'

Happily, we kept a big plastic tank topped up with fresh water. I half-filled the kettle and got it going on the stove.

While we waited, I pulled a few other useful things out of the rucksack.

'Like camping,' she observed.

'Exactly!'

'But what's the point?'

'To get some rest — both of us. We're safe here. No need to worry about people from Russia or Chicago finding us. When we return to the cottage,' I added, 'we can take turns keeping watch while one of us sleeps. Right now, though, we both need to sleep.'

She didn't disagree, and she cheered up a lot once she had a mug of hot coffee in her hand.

Noticing her give a discreet yawn, I said, 'We'll have this drink, and then get our heads down. If you're anything like me, you're ready for sleep.'

'Very ready,' she agreed.

A strong gust of wind hit the cabin and hurled a sheet of rain or spray at the window looking out over the sea. The cabin was unmoved.

Lady shivered theatrically. 'It's actually quite nice in here, isn't it?'

'I think so,' I admitted. 'I've spent many an hour, and quite a few nights, tucked away in this little cabin. Jimmy Mack, my neighbour, did a good job when he built it many years ago.'

'He has the other cottage?'

I nodded. 'He's a retired fisherman, whose family have lived in these parts for generations. I'm proud to call him my friend.'

'Friend?' she murmured, as if doubting me.

'Friend,' I said firmly. 'He's a good man.'

'Hmm,' she said. 'I've never met one like that.'

CHAPTER TWENTY-THREE

I checked the laptop I keep in the cabin to make sure that the CCTV up at the cottage was working. It was. Nothing was happening up there.

Then we talked for a little while longer. It felt like the pressure was off for the moment, and we could afford to do that. The talk wasn't always comfortable, I have to say, but it was necessary. For me, at least, it was.

'Where did you do your time?' I asked.

She looked at me with a frown.

'What jail?' I added.

'Jail! What are you talking about?'

'I'm probably talking about a high-security prison. Which one was it?'

She glared at me now as if she would like to blow me away with an assault rifle.

'OK,' I said with a shrug. 'It doesn't matter. Just making conversation.'

We sat in stony silence for a few minutes before she said, 'What do you know about me?'

'Not a lot. But I know a prison tat when I see one. You've been inside. What was it for — murder?'

'Homicide sounds better.'

'Mmm. So where were you?'

'Supermax in Florence, Colorado.'

I shook my head. 'I don't think so.'

She glared at me some more.

'It's a men's prison.'

'So?'

'I don't believe you've changed gender.'

She actually smiled at that.

'You don't have to tell me, if you don't want to,' I told her grandiosely.

'That's right. I don't need to tell you one damn thing!'

It was like fencing with an angry hornet. But I'd provoked the reaction. Deliberately so. I wanted to unsettle her, in the hope that she would disclose more than she planned. The tactic had already given me some information, and I was learning more all the time.

One thing she had confirmed was what I had already worked out for myself — she had done time in prison. The tattoo on her arm had given that away. It was the sort of tat common in prisons, and often self-inflicted by people who had very little control of anything else. It was also incomplete, which was interesting. Even if she had changed her mind about it, she would probably still have finished it. I guessed there had been an interruption. Something had happened to stop work on it.

She had also admitted something else that hadn't been hard to guess — she was there for murder, or whatever you want to call it. Homicide, in her case, seemingly. She was lucky she hadn't been convicted in one of those states where they still have the mandatory death sentence for it. Perhaps she had, but it just hadn't happened yet?

Something that puzzled me in light of all this was what she was doing here, right now. How had she managed that? She was too young to have served much of a full term for murder, given that American sentencing policies are far more draconian than ours.

Given her age, it looked like she had somehow got out early. I wondered if the unfinished, perhaps interrupted, work on her tattoo supported that interpretation. Something had happened.

She hadn't escaped. That really wasn't possible from a US prison, especially the kind you were sent to if you were sentenced for homicide. Even the billionaire Mexican and Colombian drug lords can't trick, fight or buy their way out of max-security prisons.

Somehow she had got lucky. I wondered if the fact that she was connected to an organized crime outfit had had anything to do with it. Maybe. Some sort of plea bargain, perhaps? If it suits them, big organizations, even those engaged in illegal activities, can bring in big-name, highly successful lawyers. Lawyers like that can perform stunning tricks, and even get sentences overturned.

I doubted if that was what had happened in this case, though. Rescuing an apprentice assassin just wouldn't have been worth the outlay or the hassle.

Having thought all that, I still couldn't figure out how Lady had got out of jail early. It was a mystery.

'I'm tired,' Lady announced, before our discussion could go any further. 'I need to sleep.'

'Help yourself to the top bunk,' I suggested. 'There's a sleeping bag up there.'

'I need the bathroom.'

'Ah! That's going to be difficult,' I said with a grin. 'The bathroom is up at the cottage. You'll just have to manage outside, like me and Jimmy do.'

'What about washing? You don't get washed?'

'Seldom, and only in summer.'

She humphed and made for the door.

* * *

It's strange going to bed in late morning. Unnatural, unless you're a shift worker. Even so, Lady seemed as happy as I was to do it. We were both running on empty. It was time to recharge our batteries.

Sleep came easy to me. I was used to Jimmy Mack's hut, for one thing. These days, I spend more time in it than he does himself. For another, it felt safe to go to sleep there, which it wouldn't have done up at the cottage. The people hunting Lady might come to Risky Point, but they wouldn't know about the hut, and had no reason to look for a way down the cliff face.

Lady having the top bunk meant there was even less reason for me to worry. There was no way she could get down from there to launch an attack on me, if she still had that in mind, without me waking in time to defend myself.

So I slept the sleep of the very deserving for several hours, without any difficulty whatsoever. When I awoke, it was six in the evening, and I could see through the window that the light was pretty much gone. I stayed where I was, luxuriating in the comfort and warmth, until I heard her ladyship stirring aloft.

'Awake?' I whispered.

'Yes.'

I swung my legs out from underneath my sleeping bag and planted my feet firmly on the floor. I hadn't been inside the bag in case I needed to defend myself from attack. I hadn't ruled out that possibility, unlikely though it was beginning to seem by then.

I stood and stared out of the window while I ran through the immediate options facing us. It wasn't long before I concluded that it would make sense to return to the cottage now we had both rested and caught up on some sleep. Facilities here were too limited for the hut to be more than a short-term refuge.

Lady agreed heartily.

'Let's go!' she said, climbing down from her perch and stretching to get the kinks out of her frame. 'Your cottage has a bathroom, doesn't it?'

'Oh, yes! And a bath, as well as a shower.'

'That will do for me,' she said with satisfaction.

I had to smile. She seemed to really miss having a bathroom. I wondered if that was because she was used to having one, or because it was a novelty for her. Didn't they have baths and showers in American prisons?

CHAPTER TWENTY-FOUR

Back at the cottage, I made a makeshift meal out of what I could find, which wasn't a lot. I'd been on the way to do the weekly shop when Lady and friend had erupted into my life and put a stop to that. Now there was a price to be paid.

We were both hungry and able to ignore the downside of the unlikely combination that made its way on to our plates — a mixture of cheese, tinned tuna, and fried eggs and peppers. Even some stale bread crusts. Afterwards, we settled down with coffee to resume our business discussion.

'What about the Russian woman?' I asked. 'What more can you tell me about her?'

'Nothing.'

'Nothing at all?'

'No. I'm waiting for you to tell me something about her,' she said rather tartly.

It wasn't a great start. Nor was Lady's response entirely unexpected. More patience and perseverance, on my part, was called for.

* * *

Later, to try to improve things, I opened a bottle of wine and poured a couple of glasses. Lady hesitated when I pushed one towards her at the kitchen table.

'It's not serious alcohol,' I told her. 'It's just red wine. It won't kill you.'

She understood the reference. 'Not like some of the stuff I've encountered,' she admitted.

'Prison alcohol is made of anything, isn't it?'

'Just about. But it can be as bad, even worse, out on the streets. I've learned to distrust all alcohol.'

'Then don't touch this, but it's a decent wine and I'm going to have a glass.'

To be polite, she took a sip or two. But she was no drinker. I could tell that. Perhaps it was because a young, ambitious hitman, or woman, needs to be in top mental and physical condition at all times. Maybe. Who knows?

The wine didn't help. After a couple of cautious sips, Lady left hers alone, making me wish I'd opened a less expensive bottle.

We didn't get any further that evening. Lady was withdrawn, either deep in thought or just turned off, and I was less inclined to press her hard now. Taking things a little easier with her had been paying dividends, even if the going was slower than I would have liked. At least I was learning things. The trouble was that I didn't know how much time we had. The hounds of hell could be at the front door any moment.

So we did the ordinary things you do with a newly arrived house guest. I showed her the bathroom and left her to make use of the shower while I sorted out the bed in the spare room. We had another makeshift meal. Then we whiled away an hour or two before calling it a day and retiring. I didn't expect to sleep much, given that I'd already slept half the day away, but I needed some time to myself. I assumed Lady did, too.

CHAPTER TWENTY-FIVE

Day Three

The next day didn't start very well. My breakfast guest was sullen and uncommunicative. She ate an apple and drank coffee, and that was it. My offer of toast and marmalade, a staple breakfast item for so many of us Brits, was summarily rejected. So was my attempt to restart the conversation about the Russian woman.

'You know,' I said gently, 'you're going to have to trust me a bit more.'

'Why the hell should I?' she said scornfully.

'You made the point yourself not too long ago. Remember?'

Her attitude stung. It amounted to a unilateral withdrawal from our previous agreement. It also annoyed me. I admit it. Patience and understanding on my part were close to being at an end.

I picked up the landline phone and punched in the familiar number.

'Who are you phoning?' she demanded.

'Cleveland Police.'

'Cops?' she shrieked.

I switched on the loudspeaker when my call was answered and asked for DI Peart. Lady stared at me, looking apoplectic.

'Morning, Bill!'

'Is it? What do you want?'

'I was wondering what you know about the shooting in Coatham yesterday morning.'

'You shouldn't be asking me that.'

'I know, I know! You're right. An ongoing investigation, isn't it? Still, I did wonder if I might be able to help.'

'I take it you know something about it? Why am I not surprised?'

'I do. It was a failed hit, with me the target.'

There was a pause for a big intake of breath before he spoke again. My eyes were fixed on Lady, who was looking horrified and disbelieving. She seemed stunned.

'Are you at home?'

'I am.'

'Stay right there! I'm coming to see you.'

'I'll be here.'

I switched the phone off and put it down. Looking steadily at Lady, I said, 'You're going to have to learn to trust me.'

'Who was that?' she rasped, with a hacking cough, trying to clear her throat.

'A cop I know. He'll be here in half an hour.'

She pushed her chair back and made to stand up.

'Stay where you are,' I ordered, grabbing her by the wrist of her good arm.

'Or what?' she said with a sneer.

'If you have a brain, use it. What I tell him when he arrives depends entirely on what you are going to tell me now. You don't trust me? Well, OK. But this is the consequence.

'I've been patient and tried to help you, admittedly in order to get you to help me, but it isn't working. I still know next to nothing about why I was attacked yesterday.

'I need to know more, a lot more, before I do anything else for you. And without me, you're finished. You are the one who brought up the issue of trust between us. Well, you really do need to trust me now.'

She clammed up. I watched her carefully. This was make or break. It could go either way, and I was ready for whatever she chose to do.

CHAPTER TWENTY-SIX

'What do you want to know?' she said, after a moment or two.

'Everything. Either that or I tell the cops what I know, and wave you goodbye. We'll be done. I've just about had enough.'

'I won't go back,' she said slowly. 'I'll never go back. I'll kill myself first.'

'Go back where?'

'To that cell. I won't do it!' she said, the pitch of her voice rising sharply.

'OK, OK! I get the message.'

'Do you? Do you, really?'

I said I did, but she wasn't going to be stopped.

'A concrete cell about the size of your bathroom. Everything in it made of concrete, except for the steel toilet with no seat. No window. Lights on day and night. Allowed out for half an hour every twenty-four hours for exercise.

'No human being should be subjected to that, whatever they've done,' she went on. 'It was torture. Pure and simple. I'll do anything to avoid going back there.'

I took the point. Perhaps justice had been served in a manner of speaking, but, yes, it was torture. No two ways about it.

Time was pressing, though. Bill Peart would be here very soon. We needed to get on.

'How did you get out? Did you escape?'

She looked at me as if I were a simpleton. It was a struggle for her to curb the look of contempt that began to invade her face.

'Nobody escapes,' she said flatly. 'Never, ever. Alcatraz was nothing compared to that place. I got out because the Law took me out. The Law needed my services. They had a use for someone like me, a kid with street cred who knew how to use a gun.'

'The Law?'

'Cops, FBI, CIA — whoever. Department of Justice? How do I know who they were? They never told me. All I know even now is that they had the power.

'Somebody decided I could be of use to them, and got it agreed with a judge or the prison service, or whoever, that they could take me out. Then they just did it.'

It was beginning to sound like one of those plea deals they do in the States. Charges or sentence reduced, suspended, or even dropped in exchange for information or for some service rendered, or about to be rendered.

'So you were released?'

She shook her head. 'Taken out, like I said. Still in custody, though. Flown by helicopter to some secret base in the depths of nowhere — Nebraska, maybe — and told I had a choice. I could be taken back to that nice little cell right away, or I could agree to do what they wanted me to do in exchange for being allowed to live outside.'

'What did they want you to do in exchange for your freedom?'

'Freedom?' she said scornfully. 'That was never on offer. I would still be in custody. But I could live inside or outside prison for the rest of my life. It was up to me.'

I nodded as I tried to absorb the enormity of what I was being told.

'The price for living outside was what — to help stop something that was going on?'

She nodded.

'Become part of a criminal gang, perhaps? The Miskov brothers' organization, even?'

'Yeah. I didn't know it at first, but that was what it was.'

'What did they want you to do? Pass on information? Kill people?'

'All of that.'

She shrugged and looked at me in a helpless kind of way.

'It was nothing I hadn't done before, Frank. I'd been in gangs since I was in high school — before that, even. Since my dad got himself shot to bits in some drugs scene that blew up in his face.'

'And you'd used guns?'

She nodded.

'Killed people, even?'

'One or two. Only our enemies, though. Gang enemies. No civilians.'

'This was in Detroit?'

'Yeah.'

'And you got caught?'

'Eventually,' she admitted with a weary sigh. 'Everybody goes down eventually, one way or another.'

'Your mother couldn't help you out?'

'I don't remember my mom. She disappeared soon after I was born.'

There was a pause then, a moment for reflection.

'Some life you've led,' I said, shaking my head.

'Yeah. Isn't it?'

'What sentence did you get when they sent you to prison?'

'Life without parole.'

That made me blink. I hadn't expected that. It reminded me that they do things differently on the other side of the Atlantic. Here we've moved on from that kind of 'justice'.

'How old are you, Lady, if you don't mind me asking?'

'In a couple of years I'll be thirty, and not long after that fifty, sixty, seventy . . .'

'And you'd still be there.'

There for the rest of her life.

She shook her head adamantly. 'No way! I won't let that happen. I'm out, and I won't go back.'

'So it must have seemed like a miracle when somebody told you it didn't have to be like that?'

'Oh, yeah!' she said, with a wry smile. 'Just like that.'

'What did they say?'

'I was told that if I played my part well, eventually I might even be freed. My sentence would be repealed, or some such legal word for it. Pardoned, could it have been?'

I nodded. 'Possibly. So you grabbed their hand off?'

'What do you think?'

I thought she probably did, without any reservations whatsoever.

I also thought there never had been any real prospect of freedom for her. The authorities responsible for extracting her from the prison system would have hoped to get inside information on the Miskov brothers' operation for a year or two at most, but no more than that probably. The role they had offered Lady had not been one she could have been expected to survive in for long.

'It's over now, though,' she said flatly. 'I'm no use to them after what's happened. Now I'm on the brothers' death list, it's over. So I'll never be free. They find me, they'll just send me back.'

A lot of things made sense at last, and I believed her. I believed everything she'd told me.

'But I won't go back,' she repeated, staring at me. 'Never, ever!'

I believed that, as well.

CHAPTER TWENTY-SEVEN

We were still sitting there, lost in thought, coming to terms with what had been said, when a throaty engine roar and the sound of gravel being sprayed out from big wheels told me of DI Bill Peart's arrival.

Lady looked at me, panic in her eyes.

'Don't worry,' I said, touching the back of her hand lightly with my fingertips. 'I'm not going to give you up. But I need to give the police something, to avoid being their chief suspect. They'll know soon enough, if not already, that I was there when Georgi was shot.

'Just go to the bedroom, and keep out of sight. They won't be here long. An hour, at most. Probably less.'

After only the briefest hesitation, she nodded and took herself off. I got up and started washing the dishes. I didn't want Bill to notice that two people had been having breakfast.

* * *

I opened the front door and stood waiting for Bill to park his official vehicle, the standard coloured-and-patterned Volvo SUV. He had a guy with him. So it looked like being a very official visit. I preferred it when he came alone in his own ancient Jag. That would have been too much to expect this time, though. A murder inquiry. His job would be on the line if he didn't handle this properly.

'Good morning, Frank!' he called as he got out.

'Morning.'

'How are you?' he asked as he approached.

'Still standing.'

'That's good. I've brought my new colleague, Detective Sergeant Andy Robbins, along with me.'

The colleague and I nodded at each other. Then I invited them inside. We sat around the kitchen table, aka my business conference desk.

'So what's been going on?' Bill demanded.

I shrugged. 'You tell me. I set off from here yesterday, on a perfectly ordinary morning, to do my weekly grocery shop. I intended going to the Co-op in Loftus, but on the way I noticed a car that seemed to be following me. So I extended the drive, to check it out, and we both ended up in that big car park in Coatham.

'I wasn't too worried at that stage. There were two people in the car and I assumed they just wanted to talk. Possibly potential clients.'

Bill nodded, wearing a look signifying concern. The colleague stared at me as if he didn't believe a word I said. I could see I was going to have difficulties with him.

'Two people got out of the other car. Said they wanted to talk. I asked what about. The guy in charge said they wanted to know where Malkovich was.'

'Malkovich!' Bill said, shaking his head with disgust. 'I might have known.'

'Quite.' I nodded. 'Anyway, I told them I had no idea. I hadn't seen or heard of him since he left Port Holland many months ago. That wasn't good enough. He came for me. I was ready to defend myself, but he pulled a gun. So did the other guy. The first one wanted to kneecap me. Then they started arguing about whether or not to just kill me there and then. I jumped in the Land Rover and scarpered. There were gunshots, but I didn't look back.

'For a time, I assumed they would be coming after me. So I took evasive action — as much as you can in a vehicle like mine. Didn't go home. Stayed away overnight. Thought about it, and couldn't make any sense of it at all.

'It wasn't until this morning that I heard on the radio that a man had been shot dead in the car park. That was when I decided to call you.'

'Earlier would have been better,' Bill said heavily.

'Like any normal citizen,' his mate said.

I stared at him and said, 'Have you ever had a contract on your head? Have you ever experienced trying to defend yourself when people armed with guns have come to kill you personally? Have you?'

He declined to answer.

'I thought not. If you had,' I told him, 'you would know that the experience changes things, and changes you for ever. You don't necessarily head for the nearest police station at the first sign of trouble — or anywhere else sensible, for that matter — because there's a good chance you might get shot and killed on the way. You make yourself scarce, and take cover.

'Then you take time and space to work out what's happening — if you can — and to decide what you're going to do about it.'

'Be that as it may,' Bill intervened, 'you left it a bit late to contact us, Frank.'

I shrugged and lied some more. 'I didn't know anyone had been killed.'

'Yes, well. What did you make of the man who spoke to you, the one you said was in charge?'

'Tough. Mean. Used to giving orders. Smart. Well dressed, in a city suit. Late thirties. He sounded American to me. That's about it.'

'And the other one?'

'I never really noticed the other one. Much the same, I suppose, but my eyes were on the man with the gun coming for me.'

They asked for more detail, but what more could I tell them? That the second would-be assassin was a woman? I wasn't going to do that.

I said my focus had been on getting out of there alive. The argument between the two killers who had come for me created an opportunity. I took it.

They weren't satisfied. Bill looked particularly unhappy. He may have guessed that I knew more than I was saying, but he also knew that even if I did, I wasn't going to admit it. Not yet, anyway.

'Would it surprise you to hear that there was no ID on the man that was shot dead?' Detective Sergeant Robbins asked.

I shook my head. 'No, it wouldn't.'

'Why is that, Mr Doy?'

'I took them for a pair of professional criminals, hitmen probably. People in that line of business never carry much with them. It wouldn't help, could get in the way, and it might even endanger them.'

'It sounds like you know a lot about that way of life?'

I shrugged. 'It goes with the territory I work in. But I don't expect you to understand that.'

'We do know what you do for a living, you know,' he responded with a fierce glare. 'Some of it, at least. And we weren't born yesterday.'

'Then some of your questions shouldn't need asking.'

Bill waded in to prevent the obvious animosity between us getting out of hand.

'That will do for now, I think. We'll need a statement from you, of course, Frank. Come in as soon as you can. Let's get it done.'

I nodded. 'This afternoon, perhaps?'

'Fine. And you can tell me then if, in the meantime, you've remembered anything else.'

That was a shot across my bows, but I pretended not to notice.

Detective Sergeant Robbins looked as if he was about to spit, but he managed to desist. He would be angry that I hadn't been arrested. For him, probably, I was just another of the bad guys.

Fortunately for me, Bill was more nuanced. He had sensed there was more to this than met the eye, and he would want to get to the bottom of the story. To do that, he knew he needed me onside.

I decided to give him a clue, something we could follow up on later.

'Have you found the weapons that were used?' I asked him innocently.

'Yes,' he said. 'They were in the car, the BMW.'

'Oh? Perhaps a passer-by didn't want them getting into the wrong hands?'

'Yes. That must be it,' he said gravely, giving me a little nod.

I gave them both a nice smile as I showed them out of the door. The encounter could have ended badly. That it hadn't made me feel duly grateful.

CHAPTER TWENTY-EIGHT

Lady came down the stairs as soon as the police vehicle left.

'You heard?'

She nodded and gave me a wry smile. 'Thank you.'

'I meant what I said about not giving you up. Now, perhaps, we can trust each other more, and get down to working out what we're going to do?'

'That would make a lot of sense.'

'I think so,' I said, with a smile of relief.

'You know what I want,' I told her. 'I want to avoid being assassinated. I also want to know more about the Russian woman. We haven't established who she is yet, but she could be a friend of mine, in which case, I would want to do what I can to protect her.

'What I don't really know is what you want out of it. I'd like to hear more about that.'

'My needs are very simple,' Lady said. 'I want to stay alive, like you. And I want to stay free. That means keeping away from both the Miskov brothers and the feds. I would have no future with either of them.'

'Fair enough.'

'There's something else, as well. I want to get even with the brothers. I believe Georgi was following their instructions when he set out to shoot me. It wasn't just because my arm was broken. He was going to do it anyway.

'I believed that all along. There were signs, hints, that I'd picked up along the way. That was why I carried a spare gun, and was ready for him.'

She surprised me. I hadn't been expecting this. But it did make sense of a lot of things that had happened.

'What? You think they knew who, or what, you were? They'd found out you'd been planted in their organization?'

'I think so.' She nodded. 'Yeah. I think it was a set-up. I would take the rap for killing you. Georgi would fix it that way.'

'Wow!' I pushed my chair back, laced my fingers behind my head and blew out explosively. 'Lady, we've got ourselves into a helluva big fight.'

'Haven't we just?' she said with a grin. 'Think we can handle it?'

'Oh, I think so. Somehow.'

She nodded. 'Good. We're in agreement, then. Let's get started.'

* * *

I wasn't being naive, finally throwing in my lot with Lady. I was under no illusions. She wasn't a reformed character. She was what she was, and probably long had been — a self-confessed, criminal street kid capable of just about anything, especially shooting people dead. She was all of that.

No wonder the CIA, or whichever part of the US intelligence fraternity it was, had pulled her out of a high-security prison and set her to work. No wonder, either, that the Miskov brothers had been happy to recruit and — for a time — employ her. She was a talent.

She was also more than that, of course. She was a victim, a victim of her origins and the environment in which she grew up, of her criminal associates and of those charged with protecting national security in the United States of America.

Some part of what she was now was down to her, and her own bad choices and decisions, but it looked to me like that was a pretty small part. Her options had always been tightly constrained by circumstances and by other people, notably the people who had brought her into this world. Had it been otherwise, I felt, she might have been different.

Right now she was approaching a junction, another crossroads in her life. With luck, she might get through it alive — and free.

Despite, or because of, what I knew of her, I wanted her to have a chance. She was a human being, and not all bad. No way in the world did I want her to be returned to a max-security prison, there to spend decades awaiting the end of her life — or, more likely, bringing about an early end to it herself. If I could, I would help her avoid that.

Yet it wasn't only the spirit of Christian forgiveness that made me think like that. It wasn't only altruism either, or even that there was something about her that I was coming to quite like. Self-interest also came into it. I wanted to help her partly because she could help me. As Lady herself had said, together we would be stronger. So it made sense to approach this thing together, and try to get it done.

'Tell me about Zimmerman,' I suggested, thinking of all the people who might be intent on bringing her down.

'Zimmerman?' She shook her head. 'Tell me about the Russian woman first. Who's she?'

CHAPTER TWENTY-NINE

'There are three Russian women I've been involved with, one way or another, in recent years,' I said with a weary sigh.

'My, oh my! You do get around, Frank,' Lady said, fluttering her eyelids.

'Professionally, I'm talking about. They weren't what you might call actual relationships, although I did like all the women well enough.'

One rather more than the others, I might have added, but didn't.

I paused then, to get my thoughts in order. Some things were just better not said, but I had to tell Lady enough to engage her. What I told her might trigger useful recollections she hadn't thought to mention so far.

'Sasha is a lone wolf now, a former Russian spy who absconded when she fell foul of the Kremlin clique that ousted her boss from power. Another purge was starting up, it seemed, and she needed to make herself scarce. It might be her they're after.'

'A Russian spy? What on earth were you doing with her?'

'It's a long story. She'd been sent to bring down a dissident Russian oligarch, a criminal who had established himself near here. He'd bought a derelict harbour just along the coast and was using it to run guns to Islamists in the North Caucasus, as well as to do various other things that both the Russian and the UK governments wanted to bring to an end.'

'Here — of all places?' Lady said, as if the very idea defied belief, as indeed it probably did, if you hadn't been involved.

'Right here. Amazing, isn't it?'

She nodded her agreement to that.

'And you were involved because?'

'Sasha came to my door needing help. That was the start of it. After that, I just got sucked in. Anyway, no regrets. Helping her was the right thing to do.

'When she left here, Sasha wouldn't tell me where she was going or give me any way of contacting her. She said that was because she expected people to be sent after her from Moscow, and believed it would be better for us both if I had no idea where she was.'

'And you accepted that?'

'I didn't have any choice. Anyway, it seemed to make sense at the time. It didn't occur to me that not knowing might get me killed.'

'Well, it wouldn't have been me that killed you, if that's what you're thinking. I intended shooting you in the leg — not the kneecap, by the way. I know how bad that is. But I wasn't going to shoot you dead.'

'We'll never know that for sure, though, will we?' I said, with a wry grin.

She just pulled a face.

'Anyway, thinking of the Russian woman, Sasha is definitely a possibility.'

'Who else is there?'

'Two sisters, Lenka and Olga Podolsky. Their father, Leon Podolsky, is a wealthy Russian businessman based in Prague, who had developed enemies in the Kremlin and, like so many other people, found it safer not to live in Moscow.

'When I last saw him, though, he had rebuilt some bridges with the Kremlin and was anticipating a smoother ride ahead. He had even agreed to become governor of a region in Siberia, or the Russian Far East, as part of the reconciliation deal.

'Both his daughters were intimately involved in his business life, one as an IT specialist, the other as a . . . Well, something like you, I suppose. An enforcer and personal security expert. You'd get on well with her. No, perhaps not, on second thoughts!' I amended with a grin.

'Anyway, either one of the daughters, or both of them, could be being targeted now by the Podolsky family's political enemies or business rivals.'

'You make it sound just like Chicago!'

'Well, you should know. I suppose there are similarities.

'Anyway, those are the only Russian women I've been involved with.'

I paused to think about it some more, frowned, and then resumed. 'So it has to be one of them. The question is, which of 'em? I'm hoping it's one of the Podolsky sisters. Their father is well able to protect them both.'

'Are they in hiding?'

I shook my head. 'Not so far as I know.'

'It's not going to be one of them, then, is it?' Lady pointed out. 'If it was, the brothers wouldn't have needed to come to you to find her.'

I nodded. That was true.

'So it has to be the other one. Sasha, is it?'

'Yes.'

'What's her full name?'

'No idea. I know her only as Sasha. There was never time to go any further, and it didn't seem necessary anyway.'

I was telling the truth, but not all of it. It had always been far too hectic back then to worry about formalities like correct names. There had been violent deaths, murders — a number of them — and there had been ships that exploded and sank.

Above all, like now, we had been hunted, both of us, and our escapes had been narrow. It hadn't been a good time in my life. All the same, I had become attached to Sasha, and had only with reluctance accepted her need to disappear.

'And you really don't know where she went, or where she is now?'

I shook my head.

'Or have any way of contacting her?'

'None.'

'She left you with a problem, in that case,' Lady said with a chuckle. 'Nice one, Sasha!'

CHAPTER THIRTY

'Now tell me about Zimmerman,' I said. 'I need to know about him, as well as everybody else who is looking for you, and probably for me as well now.'

'Not much to tell,' she said with a shrug. 'At least, I don't know much. I know him more by reputation than anything else. I've only ever seen him once, and that was just a fleeting glance.'

'When you first mentioned him, you made him sound like the Miskovs' enforcer.'

'I guess that's what he is. He gets rid of people they don't want around anymore.'

'And he's good at that?'

'The best.' She looked at me and sighed. 'People are scared of him, scared of what he can do.'

'So they toe the line?'

She nodded.

All organizations need somebody like that, although not necessarily to actually kill people. Mostly they investigate, uncover savoury doings, find out where the money's gone. Stuff like that. I've done some of it myself. But the likes of Zimmerman are on a different scale. They're very special. What does he look like?'

She frowned as she thought about that.

'He's nothing special to look at. Just . . . well, ordinary. You wouldn't notice him in a crowd, and you wouldn't remember him later even if you did.'

I nodded. I could understand that.

'Slim, slight even, average height, short hair, quiet, middle-aged going on elderly . . .' I recited.

'You've got him! How did you know?'

'I know the type. The best ones are all like that.'

Not everyone who looks like that is one of them, of course. Far from it. But in my experience, the hard men who get things like that done are guys you wouldn't pick out in a crowd. You don't notice them. You wouldn't even know they were there until it was too late.

Memo to self — Zimmerman must be good.

* * *

'I need to make a phone call,' Lady announced. 'I don't want to, but there will be problems if I don't. My CIA handler,' she added with a shrug. 'I'm supposed to check in with him every day.'

'Oh?'

'He's the guy I called to get the passport and money, and the other stuff.'

What 'other stuff', I wondered? The gun she said she didn't collect?

She must have made a coded request for them, and perhaps other things as well, to avoid the GCHQ computer picking up on anything significant, like the word 'gun', as it scans the world's communications.

'I wondered about that,' I said thoughtfully. 'Where is he — your handler? Do you know?'

'Not exactly, but I know he's close. At least, someone is.'

'So he's not in Chicago, or Washington?'

She shook her head. 'They keep close tabs on me. Not for my protection either, although they come in useful if I am in trouble.'

'So it seems. I was surprised how fast they responded to your call for . . . what shall we call it? Logistical support? Less than two hours, and everything was in place for you.'

'Yeah. The downside is, they're so close I can scarcely breathe. If they thought I was about to run out on them, I'd probably get wiped out by a drone strike!'

'But they weren't going to stop you shooting me?'

'No. That's true.'

'An innocent civilian, in a foreign country — a friendly ally, at that?'

'Makes no difference. You would just have been more collateral damage in their war against threats to national security.'

'You'd better make the call,' I told her with a sigh. 'I'm not fond of drones.'

* * *

She invited me to listen to the call but I made myself scarce. I thought it a good opportunity to prove that I trusted her to do the right thing. Besides, I could guess how it would go. She was going to have to play for time, and persuade them to give her it.

Meanwhile, there were things I needed to do myself.

One of those things was contacting Leon Podolski.

Leon and I had been very close at one time. For a time indeed I had been his close-protection officer, security adviser and even best pal. That time had been brief. Then we had gone our separate ways, with his undying gratitude ringing in my ears. It's what Russians seem to be like. If you're an enemy, they will never forgive you. Friends are friends for life. Leon had given me a phone number that he said would always reach him if I ever wanted to call him. Now seemed a good time to put that promise to the test.

* * *

'Frank! Is it really you?'

I smiled with relief and pleasure as I heard the voice I remembered so well.

'Yes, it is. Hello, Leon. How are you?'

'The same, just the same.'

Busy, fit and well, in other words, I thought with an affectionate smile. Probably richer, as well. Same old Leon.

'Is something wrong, Frank? I can't believe this is just a social call. If it is, I am very happy to hear from you. But if there is trouble, how can I help?'

Yep! Same old Leon. Straight to the point.

'There is trouble, Leon. It's blown up over the past couple of days. It involves Russians and Americans, and I'm wondering if you might be able to help.'

'Tell me.'

* * *

Leon Podolsky was a remarkable man, with an oligarch's resources and business interests, and with extensive contacts in the shadows of the Russian political and criminal worlds in and around which he necessarily moved. With a business hub in Prague and a family safely ensconced in Geneva, he divided his time between those cities and Moscow, the UK, Montenegro and anywhere else he happened or needed to be.

More to the point, I regarded him as one of the good guys. I had saved his life once or twice, in a desperate time, and he had saved mine. So our relationship was special, and for life.

I told him what had happened and where things stood now, mostly in the hope that he might be able to help me help Sasha. She needed to be warned, and I also hoped that he might be able to discover who it was that was hunting her. Such things were beyond me and my capabilities, but Leon Podolski knew his way around the Kremlin labyrinth. He was also a wheeler-dealer like no other.

Given how little I could tell him about Sasha, it seemed like a daunting commission. But Leon wasn't daunted.

All he said was, 'Leave it with me, Frank. I'll see what I can do, and then get back to you.'

CHAPTER THIRTY-ONE

'So how did your phone call go?' I asked Lady.

'Fine. Good. Felix was OK with what I told him.'

'Felix?'

'My handler. Or case officer. Whatever you want to call him.'

'That's his name?'

'It's what he calls himself when he's dealing with me. I have no idea what his real name is. Maybe that's it.'

Not in my estimation. Nor in Lady's either, it sounded like. Long-time undercover intelligence operatives and handlers probably struggle to recall their real names.

'And he was OK about what, exactly?'

'Me shooting Georgi. I told him it had been him or me, and that the brothers had probably found me out. He said it wasn't good, but he understood. He would make arrangements to have me brought out, and would let me know when they were ready. Meantime, I should stay low, and stay in touch.'

'What did you say to all that?'

'I thanked him very much, of course.' She shrugged. 'I ain't going back, though. And they're not taking me back. Fuck that! They pull me out, I know where I'll end up — right back in the fucking slammer!'

I thought she was right about all of that. Her value to them was at an end now, the same as with the Miskovs. The operation would be aborted. Felix could go on leave, and Lady back to her concrete cell.

The CIA's priority would be to get her off the street, and back where they believed she belonged, to avoid the risk of what they had done being revealed to the public gaze. Minimizing embarrassment to themselves, and possible public censure, would galvanize them. I didn't believe they would wait for her to turn up, either. They would come looking for her.

'You don't know where Felix is?' I asked again.

She shook her head, and said, 'Somewhere pretty darned close. That's all I can tell you. Here, in this country, and probably not far away from where we are right now.'

That was my guess, too, given how fast she had been re-supplied when she had put in her demands.

'Does he know where you are?'

'Not from me. No way! I just told him I would lie low until I heard about the pick-up.'

She would get the details, I supposed, when she checked in with him on one of her scheduled calls. So we had a little time before then to work out what we were going to do.

I would just have to hope Leon came up with something soon. If not, I could see us having to move again. It felt like we were fast becoming sitting ducks, here at Risky Point. All our adversaries would know we were here.

* * *

Felix wasn't the only one with an interest in Lady, of course. In front of him, in the queue of people looking for her, was Lucas and the backup team. They had a head start on Felix, as well, but Felix would probably have more technology to help him search. It was going to be a close-run race between them to get here first.

Then there was DI Bill Peart, of the Cleveland Police. I hadn't forgotten him. Nor had I forgotten Zimmerman, the Miskovs' go-to guy when they wanted something dirty doing.

The queue was a long one. Whoever it was that got here first, though, the result would be the same. Unless we came up with something really good, I couldn't see that Lady needed to fear being returned to her prison cell. None of the parties looking for her would allow that to happen. Only Bill Peart, if he ever caught up, would entertain the thought of her staying alive even.

I wondered if Lady had reached the same conclusion all by herself, and I decided she almost certainly had. She was pretty smart and she was streetwise. She knew these people, and plenty like them, and had done all her life. She knew what happened to worker ants and bees when they reached the end of their useful lives. They were terminated. She would have seen it happen too often to be in any doubt about what her own prospects were.

So, then? What did Lady have in mind, I wondered? She didn't strike me as the kind of gal who was just going to give up and go quietly. She was a survivor, and she wanted revenge. She had told me that herself. And somehow, she must think me capable of helping her achieve whatever her immediate aims were.

And after that? I didn't know, but I imagined she would be planning a disappearing act. Sasha had shown me how that could be done. I wondered if Lady was as capable as her.

CHAPTER THIRTY-TWO

Leon got back to me surprisingly fast. But, then, that was typical of him. He waited for nothing and nobody. Since the Kremlin had stopped making an enemy of him, he must have become a very valuable asset.

'It's not good, Frank, I have to tell you. But it could be worse. The woman you asked about is almost certainly Alexandra Kuznetsova. She disappeared while on active service in your region. Her body was not found, which meant her file was not closed, but there has been no official contact with her since then.'

'Has anyone looked for her?'

'Not officially. But a certain faction within the service retains an interest. You probably know how these things work, Frank.'

'I do. They'll never stop looking, will they?'

'Never.'

The service he was talking about was military intelligence, the GRU. Leon was ex-Spetsnaz, possibly even ex-GRU, and obviously had connections there still. He was far too useful a guy to have been written off when he decided to relocate his business hub to the Czech Republic for reasons of personal safety.

'Have there been any . . . sightings of her?'

'A possible in Venezuela. But it's not certain.'

'Venezuela?'

That was a surprise. I could have understood New Zealand, or somewhere even more tranquil in the South Pacific, but Venezuela?

'You know how it is, Frank. When all is in turmoil, it is easy to hide and find refuge. In a peaceful, stable community a newcomer stands out.'

'True.'

I might have added that if you're used to mayhem and confusion, ordinary decent life can probably seem a bit dull, as well.

'How firm was the sighting?'

'I can only say, from my own experience, that if it hadn't been firm, it wouldn't have been reported. Nobody wants to look a fool. It is too dangerous!' he added with a chuckle.

'So she's alive, probably?'

'I believe so, yes.'

It was good to have that assurance. Coming from Leon, it meant a lot.

'As for the other woman you asked about, I will make enquiries amongst my contacts in Chicago to see what they know of her.'

It wouldn't be any good asking peaceful, law-abiding people in Chicago, but I knew Leon wouldn't be thinking of doing that. Even though he was a legitimate businessman, he would have plenty of contacts amongst the other sort as well. Perhaps he could shake something loose.

'Frank, there is one other thing you should know. It may be relevant.' He paused before saying, 'Red Star still exist.'

'Really?'

'Oh, yes. Their *kvost* is still alive and active, just as in the early days of the Soviet Union. I believe they, too, are in Venezuela. Possibly they are pursuing Kuznetsova, or she is pursuing them. I don't know.'

That gave me something more to think about. It was because of the personal threat to Sasha from Red Star, one of those extremist groups forever scheming and agitating behind the scenes in the Kremlin, that Sasha had defected and gone into hiding. I hoped it was just a coincidence that they, too, were in Venezuela.

'That's very helpful, Leon. Thanks a lot.'

'It's not much, but at least it's something. It's a start. Do you need more practical help there on the ground, Frank? If you do, let me know. I can have people there with you in less than one hour. Perhaps half that.'

'Thanks again, Leon. Things are OK for now, but I'll certainly keep your offer in mind.'

Afterwards, I wondered if he still had *The Chesters*, an ancient country house in north Northumberland that had become his IT base in the UK. It sounded very much like it, if he could get a team here so fast. Perhaps I would get to see it, and him, again one of these days.

On second thoughts, I rather hoped not. My life was hazardous and chaotic enough without reinvolving myself with the Podolskys.

CHAPTER THIRTY-THREE

'Do you have any weapons?' Lady asked.

That took me back a bit. It wasn't a question anyone had ever addressed to me before, not in my own home at least.

'Weapons?'

'Guns.'

'A shotgun. It's usually locked away, but just now I'm keeping it next to the front door. You may have noticed?'

She shook her head impatiently. 'I'm not talking about a gun for shooting pigeons off the fence!'

I just looked at her and shrugged, but I knew well enough what she was talking about.

'A guy like you, who does what you do for a living, doesn't have any guns? You expect me to believe that?'

'It's different in this country. Illegal.'

'So I've heard,' she said with a weary sigh.

'Even the cops don't have guns. The ordinary cops, at least.'

She nodded, left it a few moments and then said, 'So what should I do when Lucas and his pals come? How should I defend myself if you're not around, or if they've shot you first? Tell me that!'

She had a point. In the nature of things, I couldn't always be by her side. There were going to be times when she was alone, alone with a broken arm, and possibly facing extremely dangerous men.

There wouldn't be any messing either. They would be in and out — a couple of shots, one more to the head to be sure. Lady slain, and the Chicago guys exiting and heading for the nearest airport. Job done.

'Well, you could shout at them, or spit and tell them you've got Aids or Ebola, or something. That might work.'

'Yeah, yeah. Very funny.'

But she wasn't amused, not at all.

I mulled things over. The word *trust* came to mind again, or rather, *trust?* with a question mark. I can't deny it. Time had moved on, and so had our relationship. But, still, could I trust her — really, really trust her?

Yet I knew I had to. I simply had to trust her now. We'd come too far together. We'd painted ourselves into a corner. The option of not trusting her was no longer open to me.

'Give me a couple of minutes,' I said, getting to my feet.

* * *

'I can lend you this,' I said, passing her the Glock 19 pistol that I kept illegally for special occasions — such as when all else failed, or when I travelled abroad. In European countries, even the traffic wardens carry guns. So guess what professional criminals have to help them conduct their business! And I don't even want to talk about the Americas.

She took the pistol and ran expert eyes and fingers over it. 'Is it clean?' she demanded, meaning, was it connected to any crime scene?

'It's clean.'

Inspection complete, she pointed the gun at me. 'Bam!' she said.

I nodded, unimpressed. 'We take guns seriously, over here,' I told her. 'They're not toys.'

'Yeah, yeah.'

She played around with the Glock some more and then said, 'So it's never been used?'

'I didn't say that. It's never been connected to a crime scene. That's what I meant.'

'So you've never shot anybody? In your role as a security guy, bodyguard or whatever the hell it is you do?'

'I didn't say that either. My policy has always been to replace any gun that has been used — when it has been — with another just like it.'

'You're a cautious guy,' she said, with grudging approval. 'That's what I do myself.'

That was when I suddenly realized I had done her a disservice by leaving behind the guns used in the Coatham car park. At least two of them, including the murder weapon, carried Lady's fingerprints.

But that couldn't be helped. Not now. And back then other considerations had been far more pressing. Lady's safety had not been a priority for me then, not after what she had very nearly done to me, and what she had actually done to her boss.

'Thanks,' she said, putting the Glock down beside her. 'I'll look after it,' she added with a wry smile.

'Please do. It's the only one I've got right now.'

CHAPTER THIRTY-FOUR

Day Five

It was a hard, bright morning when Lucas came to my door. He came alone, but only from as far as the SUV parked on my gravel patch. I could see other faces staring out from the vehicle when I opened the door.

'Frank Doy?'

He was a little guy, a good bit shorter than me and much slighter as well. I wasn't fooled. He had a hard face and mean eyes that looked as if they had seen the worst that can happen and hadn't blinked.

I nodded. 'That's me.'

'Lady Day here?'

'Who?'

He looked steadily at me and said, 'We know you've been fooling around with her, Doy. Send her out — now!'

Little he might be, but I had no doubts about his power or his capabilities. Lady was right to be worried about him.

'While you're at it,' he added, conversationally, 'you can tell me where the Russian woman is.'

I shook my head and said, 'You're out of order, talking to me like that.'

'This ain't your fight, buddy,' he added. 'But you can sure as hell make it yours, if that's what you want. We don't want you, Doy. Not now. We did at one time, but not now. It's her we want. Let's do a deal. She comes with us, and you stay right here in your little house.'

I think it was the scorn and derision in his voice that stiffened my resolve. There was no way in the world that I would accept even passing the time of day with a man who spoke so disparagingly of my home, me and my whole life.

'It's not going to happen, Lucas,' I told him. 'Your best plan is to leave — now!'

'Like that, is it?' he said easily.

I nodded.

'Well, know this. We're coming for you — both of you!'

Suddenly, a gun appeared in his hand. He'd caught me cold. I hadn't expected things to degenerate as fast as this.

'When I say now,' he said quietly, 'I mean right now. Get her out here!'

The angle of the gun declined. I realized with a sickening feeling what was supposed to come next. Kneecapping seemed to be a speciality of these people from Chicago.

There was a sharp explosion from somewhere behind me. Lucas yelped and stepped back. His arm dropped, and the gun went with it.

'You heard the man!' Lady said, pushing me aside. 'On your way, Lucas. You'd better go while you've still got legs to take you.'

Gritting his teeth, Lucas looked past me with an expression of agony and fury combined. Before he could make any attempt to even things up, I reached down and wrenched the gun from his shattered hand.

He snarled at me. I spun him round and hustled him back to the waiting vehicle. Doors had opened but nobody had actually emerged from it yet. Wise counsel had no doubt taken note of the gun pointed at Lucas's head.

'Wait!' Lady snapped.

Both Lucas and I stood still.

‘Stay in the vehicle, boys!’ Lady said, pointing her gun for emphasis. ‘Turn this thing around and get out of here. When you reach the end of the track, stop and wait for Lucas. He’ll be walking along to meet you.’

‘And while you’re doing all that,’ I told them, ‘I’ll be phoning the cops. It won’t take them long to get here.’

‘Now, go!’ Lady concluded.

Their vehicle was turned round and set off along the track. Lucas followed on foot, head high but no doubt in agony from his broken hand, as well as from the psychological damage Lady had inflicted on him.

We stood waiting and watching until he reached the SUV and got inside. Then we watched it drive away.

‘Nice shot,’ I said, as we turned away and headed back indoors.

‘Thanks.’

‘You’re welcome. I was worried I’d left it too late to get involved.’

I shook my head. ‘No. Perfect timing.’

‘They’ll be back.’

‘You think?’

She nodded. ‘If they go home to Chicago now, empty handed, it won’t be long before Lucas has something far worse happen to him.’

‘In that case, we’d better get down to business.’

CHAPTER THIRTY-FIVE

'So far as I'm concerned,' I told her, 'you could clear off now if you want to. I've got what I needed to know. It's Red Star, looking for Sasha, that have taken out the contract on me. They know I was once associated with her, and will assume I know where she is now. They must be desperate,' I added with a shrug.

'So there's nothing to hold you here. For your own sake, you should go while you can, before things heat up anymore.'

Lady was humming and singing to herself as she cleaned the pistols, the one we'd taken from Lucas and the Glock I had loaned her. It was a difficult, frustrating thing to do one-handed, but she seemed to be managing. She actually appeared to be more content than she had been so far, perhaps even happy. Guns were obviously her thing. Both using and looking after them. Her disarming Lucas had been something to behold, and the current clean-up made clear that she knew what she was doing in the aftermath as well.

I quite liked hearing her sing, even if the song was a sad one about stormy weather and a man that got away. It sounded vaguely familiar. I must have heard it somewhere. A blues number, I guessed. Possibly even one sung by her namesake. For a moment, I regretted not knowing anything about that kind of music. It might have been useful in talking to her, as well as educational for me.

'There's your arm, of course,' I said, still thinking of the best course for her to take now that Lucas and his team had appeared on the scene. 'That will handicap you.'

'It hasn't so far, has it?' she countered swiftly.

I shook my head. 'I envy you being ambidextrous.'

'That's not natural. I'm right-handed. It's just that I've spent a lot of time working on my weaker hand.'

An awful lot of time, I thought. An incredible amount of time, and perseverance, to be able to bring her weaker hand up to be able to shoot like that with it. Twice now, as well. First, Georgi. Now, Lucas.

'So you want to be rid of me? Is that what you're saying?'

'No, I'm not saying that.'

'I wouldn't blame you if you did. You had a good life till I arrived.'

'Stop it!' I said with irritation. 'That's not what this is about, and you know it.'

'So what is it about, Frank? Tell me.'

'I'm wondering what the best thing for you is.'

'Huh,' she said, making her scepticism clear.

'Look, I've got what I needed out of our deal. First, you've told me what I wanted to know about the attack on me. I now know what it was about, and who launched it.

'Second, I know now that the real target was Sasha. That's who they're after. I didn't even know if she was alive, but Leon has told me he believes she probably is. If she's still in Venezuela, she's as safe there, in all that chaos, as she would be anywhere on the planet. Nobody will find it easy to find her there.

'So my interests are satisfied. I could even bring the police up to date now, and sort things out with them. What I'm wondering is if there's any point in you hanging around here any longer. You could get away before anyone else comes looking for you. The world's a big place.

'First, though, we need to get you back to the hospital, to have them check on your arm. But maybe then it would be best for you to disappear and find somewhere safe. Make a new life for yourself. No need to wait for Felix to put you back in prison, or somebody to shoot you. What do you say?'

She worked on polishing the guns for a minute or two before replying. Then she said, 'I doubt I could do that. Disappear, like you said. I'm not too bothered about the Miskovs, but do you have any idea how many people the CIA employ? A hundred thousand? And how many more they retain on a contract basis, and how many they pay good money to for information? Do you?'

It was a point. The answer to her questions could well be close to seven figures, worldwide. That was a hell of a lot of people to be looking for you.

'So you're saying the CIA could find you?'

'Yeah. I am.'

She had nothing more to say. She'd said her piece.

'Even so,' I insisted, 'it still might be worth trying.'

She shook her head. 'We keep on misunderstanding each other, Frank. What I'm saying is that Felix would never stop looking for me for as long as he works for the CIA. Then, when he retires, dies or whatever, someone else would pick up the file and continue looking. That's how it works. The file would never be closed. I'd never be free of them.'

I could see her point. 'Felix' was just the label attached to her handler. If the guy currently in office moved offstage, someone would take his place and inherit the name.

Felix was a unit in a vast organization, not the personal name of a human being.

All the same, there was a particular person there right now. There was a person running things and taking decisions. Felix wasn't a robot or a computer. And the thing about a person is that he or she is human. That means you can negotiate with him or her, and possibly even do a deal.

After all, wasn't that what Lady had done with me? And she'd been in an impossible starting position — spreadeagled on the tarmac with a broken arm, the boss she'd shot dead lying beside her, me livid with her, and her with no money, passport, weapon, or anything else. But she'd done it. She'd got herself a deal.

'Yet if you ran, you couldn't be taken back to a prison cell. With luck, you could even stay outside permanently. Isn't that worth thinking about?'

She shrugged and carried on polishing pistols that didn't need any more polishing.

'OK.' I said with a sigh. 'You don't think so.'

'You got that right.'

'Well, how about this? Maybe we could do a deal with Felix, one that would keep you free.'

CHAPTER THIRTY-SIX

'What do you have in mind?' she asked, looking up with a smile. 'Having me sing for them? Maybe front a blues band?'

'That's an idea,' I said, smiling back. 'I hadn't thought of that.'

'So what were you thinking?'

'How about if we proposition Felix — offer him crucial information that will help him bring down the Miskov brothers and seriously reduce Russian illegal activities in the US, in exchange for him looking the other way when you depart, and then forgetting about you? What do you think?'

She sighed. 'Where were you, Frank, when they were giving out brains in your home town?'

'You don't like the idea?'

'Oh, I like it fine. It's just that it's cloud cuckoo land!'

'Not necessarily. I want you to think about it very carefully. What do you have to offer that would excite Felix sufficiently for him to want to do a deal with you? Take your time. Work it out. There may be something that will make them foam at the mouth with anticipation.'

'Yeah. Right. What was it you said about going back to the hospital?'

'Is that what you want to do?'

'It's a more useful thing to do than sitting here talking fantasy with you.'

I laughed. 'OK. Come on, then. Get your coat!'

* * *

I wasn't too disappointed. I just put the conversation aside for the moment. There were plenty of other things to think about and to do.

As we left for the hospital, I reminded Lady that Lucas and his pals were likely to be back. They might not have gone away for good.

'They might not have gone away at all,' she said. 'Just far enough to be out of sight. What do you want to do about it?'

'Stay here, for now. We have cards to play while we're here. If we leave, we won't have them.'

'Oh? What do you have in mind?'

'There are things we can do from here, like negotiating with Felix and waiting to see if my pal Leon comes up with anything. And, if things are desperate, I could get the cops out here in no time at all, now that Bill Peart knows about the threat to me.'

'Hmm. He doesn't know about me, though, does he?'

'He doesn't need to. You're like . . .'

'Your secret weapon?'

'Yes. That's it!'

Laughing, I shut the car door after her once she was inside, pleased her sense of humour had survived.

* * *

The hospital dealt with things briskly. They replaced the temporary splint with a fibreglass casing, rather than a traditional, heavy plaster cast, and said things were looking fine. Just carry on as you are doing, they said. They didn't say anything about not shooting guns. So she didn't have to lie and tell them she wouldn't.

Then we left.

* * *

It was still daylight when we got back to Risky Point, and things there looked just as we'd left them. I wondered about the night, though. It was hard to believe we would be unmolested that night. Lucas and his team had had time to regroup and would surely have spent it organizing themselves. They would be back.

I began packing a rucksack.

'What?' Lady said.

'We may not be staying here,' I told her. 'There could be some heavy artillery on the way. It could be like the OK Corral here tonight.'

'So what do you want to do?'

'Be ready to move down to the hut, if necessary.'

'They could be watching. They would just follow us.'

I shook my head. 'Not the way we'd go — if we have to.'

I finished what I was doing. Then I called Bill Peart and told him what had happened earlier that day, and what I suspected might happen that night.

'So now you're asking for police protection?'

'I suppose I am. For both my cottage and Jimmy Mack's. And for both of us, as well, if we're here.'

'Oh, boy! You're thinking of leaving, are you?'

'Not unless I have to, but I don't know what might happen tonight. There were men here with guns this morning, and I don't fancy meeting them again. If I'm not here,' I added, 'you know where I keep my spare key. Feel free to use it.'

'Is that all you can tell me?'

'There isn't much more at the moment, but I can tell you what the armed gang want.'

'Go on.'

Ignoring Lady's look of horror, I said, 'It's to do with that Russian business the other year. Basically, they're looking for Sasha, the Russian woman. Remember her? For some reason I don't begin to understand, they believe they can get to her through me. They can't, because I have no idea where she went when she left here, and I have no means of contacting her, either.'

'I thought you said there was a contract on you?'

'There is. That's it! This Chicago gang picked it up. They were going to shoot me a bit at a time until they got the information they wanted.'

'I see,' Bill said, his tone heavy with disbelief.

I couldn't really blame him.

'What do you know about this gang? Who are they?'

'Well, I'm guessing it's a Russian contract. I can't imagine anyone else being interested in Sasha. The people who picked it up are from Chicago. They work for the Miskov brothers, who are of ethnic Russian descent and run an organized crime outfit there. And that's about all I do know.'

I didn't mention CIA involvement. That would really have done his head in.

'It sounds to me like something for the security service.'

'Yes. Probably.'

I thought he would be relieved to hear that. It meant it wasn't all going to be down to Cleveland Police, although they would have to be involved.

After a lengthy pause for further reflection, he said, 'But we need to have a firearms team on standby.'

'Yes. That would be good.'

'Meanwhile,' he said with a heavy sigh, 'my best advice is to get well away from Risky Point, but keep me informed as to your whereabouts.'

'That's the plan.'

'OK. Good. I'll see what can be done.'

Bill rang off, obviously in a pretty foul mood. Something was going on that he didn't understand, and quite rightly he resented it. Not for the first time, I'd landed him in the middle of something toxic. And now he had to do something about it.

The only good thing was that I'd given him enough to know this wasn't really, or only, police business. It had to be passed upstairs, and then probably on to higher authority still. So he might be able to watch the football on the telly, after all.

* * *

Lady was looking daggers at me. I didn't care. We couldn't go on any longer like we had been doing. This was too big for little old me to handle, even with the help of a one-armed hitwoman.

I finished packing a few more essentials. Lady watched in sullen silence, possibly wondering if this was the time she should split and make her own way out of here before the uniforms arrived to lock her up.

A few minutes later I heard engine noise and saw headlight beams shining along the track. It didn't look good.

'Come on!' I snapped. 'We're leaving.'

I waited until I saw men spilling out of the vehicle and then speed-dialled Bill Peart. I didn't get him, but I left a message on his phone. 'They're here!' it said. 'The gang from Chicago.'

CHAPTER THIRTY-SEVEN

In the back porch, I grabbed a powerful battery lamp from a shelf, switched it on and stooped to lift the trapdoor that was disguised and built into the floor. I clattered down the steps and turned to help Lady down after me.

'What the hell is this?' she demanded as she followed me reluctantly.

'The emergency exit,' I snapped.

I got her down, and closed the heavy trapdoor after her. Then I handed her another lamp, one I kept down there, and led the way down a flight of stone steps and into a tunnel. That took us underneath Jimmy Mack's cottage, and on to emerge from a timber doorway in the cliff face. We passed through and I secured the door. Then we stood for a moment, while we caught our breath and took stock.

The next phase of the journey wouldn't be easy for Lady. You really needed two hands for the scramble ahead of us. I could see her looking askance at our situation, and perhaps holding her breath. Unlike guns, heights were not her thing.

'Don't worry,' I said in a cheerful voice. 'It's not as bad as it looks.'

She drew herself up to her full height of just over five feet and — I could just make out through the gloom — glared indignantly at me. I would have given her a hug of encouragement but for the fear that she might push me off into space.

We were about thirty feet down from the top of the cliff, and something like that distance laterally away from the usual route down it. The light was too poor for the bottom of the cliff to be visible, which was just as well. Thankfully, our position couldn't be seen from anywhere nearby. We were standing on a small promontory tucked away at a point where the cliff face was recessed in a narrow gully. While we stood there, we couldn't be seen by anyone who wasn't out to sea in a boat, but we couldn't stay there. We had to get down to the hut.

Not being able to see where she might fall was going to make it easier for Lady to get across to the fixed rope, and the usual path.

It was still a struggle to do it. I have to admit that. Touch and go, even. Fortunately, it was a route that I had worked on a few times. I knew the handholds and footholds along the way well enough and could nurse Lady along gently even in the poor light. The lamps we'd been carrying might have been a help, but they'd been left in the tunnel. Useful as they could have been, I'd felt we couldn't afford to risk using them. The last thing we needed was for Lucas and his gang to have any idea where we were.

To my relief, we managed to scramble across without catastrophe. Lady grabbed the rope as if it were a lifebelt in the middle of the ocean. Thankfully, she said nothing, and in the semi-darkness I couldn't see if she was glaring at me, which I guessed she was.

Sensibly, she concentrated on keeping her balance and focused on the descent. That was quite hard enough. The rope helped a lot. Without it, coping one-handed would have been impossible. I stayed close enough to grab her if she slipped.

I wasn't needed. We made it to the foot of the cliff without mishap and crunched our way over the shingle to the hut.

I could have been worried about the cottages and what was happening up aloft, but I wasn't. Unlike people, property can always be fixed. That was how I looked at it. Thankfully, we were out of the firing line, and so was Jimmy Mack. Nothing else really mattered right now.

CHAPTER THIRTY-EIGHT

While I heated water for coffee on the camping stove, Lady lay slumped on the lower bunk and stared at something I couldn't see. Either she was doing some deep thinking or she was just emotionally and physically exhausted by the climb down the cliff face. I left her to it. Even for an apprentice hitman, and tough kid that she was, she had been through a lot lately.

Coffee brought her round. She sat up and said, 'I've been thinking.'

'We all have to do that from time to time,' I told her with a grin. Then I ducked to avoid the poisoned frown she threw at me.

'About what you said.'

'Oh?'

'Reaching a deal with Felix would be great, if it could be done.'

I nodded with satisfaction. This sounded like a good start.

'But I don't know how it could be done,' she added, with a despairing note in her voice. 'I mean, what can I offer him?'

'Oh, there'll be something,' I said airily. 'Bound to be. Lots of things, probably. What you have to remember is what Felix's priority is. It's not you personally. That's for sure!

'You're just a means to an end. So are the Miskov brothers, for that matter. His priority, and the CIA's, will be to stop or reduce Russian troublemaking in the US. That's what this is all about. It's why they sprang you from jail.'

'So?'

'So we need to work out what you have, or know, that will help Felix do his job. There's bound to be something. It really is that simple, believe me.'

'Money?' she asked, after a moment's thought.

I shook my head. 'The CIA has more than it knows what to do with. Hell, they buy and sell entire countries! They always have done.'

'The Miskovs are interested in money.'

'I'm sure they are, but so what? We're not worried about them. At least, we won't be once their people are gone from Risky Point.'

Lady went back to thinking again, which was what I wanted her to do. There might not be anything we could offer Felix, but, if there was, it was Lady who was going to have to come up with it. She just needed space to think about it.

'I'm going to take a look outside,' I told her, raising my mug to drain the last of the coffee. 'I want to see what the tide's doing.'

She nodded and continued staring at the ceiling.

* * *

It was cold outside. The hut had become reasonably warm from our presence and the heat from the camping stove. It made me wonder if the global-warming campaigners had thought yet of ridding the planet of six or seven billion human beings to slow things down. It would surely make a difference. Someone else would have to point that out to them, though. I had enough to do.

Now that my eyes had better adjusted to the dim light, I could see that the tide wasn't doing anything special. It was a quiet night down here. Without any fanfare or drama, the sea was just easing its way in, deepening and reaching higher up the cliffs as I watched. Scarcely daring to hope, I wondered if it was quiet up on top of the cliff as well. I could hear nothing from down here.

Had Lucas just taken his gang away when they found nobody was home? Or had they ransacked and torched the place before they left? Had Bill Peart got officers there in time to make a difference? All I could do was shrug and resolve not to dwell on questions I couldn't answer. There was no point.

Meanwhile, the tide was still coming in. The sea was pressing its case, relentlessly probing for weakness in the cliff wall and the rock pedestal at its base. Each wave brought it slightly higher up our little beach, and then there followed the seething, hissing sound of it pulling back through the shingle.

Of weakness in the land's defences there was no doubt. The cliffs had been retreating for millennia, if not longer. The abrupt exit from the tunnel we had just used to get here was proof of that. At one time, the tunnel would have led to a path, possibly even a staircase, down the cliff face. Then erosion had taken down a whole section of cliff, path and staircase along with it, leaving Jimmy Mack and me to make do with the hazardous route we usually used.

I smiled, wondering if Jimmy knew of the tunnel. Probably not, or he would have mentioned it. Perhaps, though, he'd heard something of it as folklore or oral tradition, from tales spun long before he'd arrived on the planet. It was entirely possible. That was how he had known of the way up the cliff from the beach. It was a fragment of ancient knowledge that had saved my life, and Sasha's, a few years earlier.

As for the tunnel, it was only recently that I had discovered it myself. Just a few months ago, even though I had lived here for quite a few years. The discovery had been through pure accident. One day, out in Jimmy's coble, I had spotted something odd in the cliff face. On investigation, back on land, that had turned out to be the heavily weathered and largely rotted remains of the exit doorway. Seething with curiosity, and no little trepidation, I had entered the tunnel and followed it back to its starting point, which happened to be under the floor of my back porch.

I was pretty sure by then that the tunnel would have been built at about the same time as the cottage itself, in the heyday of the late-eighteenth-century smuggling boom. That was when evading the Revenue was a major part of the economy for folks along this coast.

Runswick Bay, a town just a few miles south of Risky Point, is known to be honeycombed with smugglers' tunnels, and one had been discovered just a few years ago in a house near Boulby, even closer to Risky Point. So there we were — with a potential tourist attraction I had decided to keep quiet about.

Since the discovery, I had expended time and effort secretly repairing some of the damage that time and erosion had wrought. Debris had been removed and timbers replaced. The roof had been shored up in places and the floor smoothed out. The work had appealed to my imagination. I had kept it quiet because I had thought there might come a time when the tunnel could prove useful to me. Today that day had come.

Smiling to myself, eased by my reflections, I returned to thinking again about what, if anything, Lady might have to offer Felix. Ideally, it would be something fundamental, something infrastructural, to the illicit Russian presence and capability in the United States. What would it look like? And what might Lady Day know about it?

My enthusiasm faded as I dismissed one possibility after another, until I was left with nothing at all. It was time to talk to Lady again, and to hope she had come up with something herself.

CHAPTER THIRTY-NINE

'I haven't thought of anything,' Lady said, as soon as I got back inside the hut. 'I don't think there is anything.'

'Well, let's just check.' I took off my jacket and slung it over a chair.

'OK. If that's what you want to do. What's happening out there, by the way?'

'The tide's coming in. Seagulls are coming with it. I heard a foghorn way out to sea somewhere.'

'That it? What about up at your cottage?'

'No idea. I'm not even thinking about that.'

I yawned to give an impression of a lack of concern that I didn't really have and sat down. 'I've been doing some thinking, as well.'

She looked suspiciously at me.

'Let's go back to some basic facts and principles,' I suggested. 'We can start with what Felix wants. As I said before, it's not you he wants. It's not really me, or Sasha, the Russian woman, either. It's cracking down on illegal Russian activities in the United States of America. That's what he wants.

'I was wrong when I said before that it wasn't even the Miskovs he was after. I've changed my mind about that. The

Miskovs will be in the frame, because they're working for Red Star. And it's Red Star that he really wants.

'He won't care about Red Star hunting Sasha. That's Russian business. But he will care about them using United States territory and people to do it, and they're doing that because they have an effective strike force in Chicago — the Miskov brothers. If he brings them down, it's a big strike against illegal Russian activity in America.

'So what we have to do is come up with something that will help him do that.'

'And that's it? That's what you've been thinking?' Lady said with a scornful smirk.

'Yes, it is.'

'While you were out on the beach, watching the tide come in, huh?'

'Yep.'

'That's pretty good, Frank. Maybe I should go out on the beach myself, 'cos I've got diddly-squat just lying here.'

She sat up. I was pleased to see that at least she was engaging with me. Good. I needed that. The sarcasm didn't put me off at all.

'So now you'll want to know what I know that could be damaging to the brothers?' she said.

'Right. Let's run through the possibilities.'

'Easier to tell you what I don't know. Like, I don't know where they keep their money.'

'Doesn't matter,' I said, shaking my head. 'Just keep talking. Let's brainstorm this.'

She sighed and said, 'It's probably invested in property and with offshore finance companies, like other big crime gangs do. Plenty of so-called legitimate billionaires, too.'

'Probably. Forget about money for now, though. Let's start with some basics. Do you know where they live, for example? And how many brothers there are?'

She screwed her face up in thought. 'How many? I only ever saw two, Boris and Yuri, but I know there's more. One more, at least. He's somewhere in South America.'

'Leave him aside for the moment, as well. Where do the two you've actually seen live?'

'They have mansions somewhere outside the city, but I don't know where exactly.'

'Have you met them?'

'Not really. Not by myself, I mean. I just went along with Georgi to meetings once or twice. We met downtown, in a hotel they own.'

She was trying hard. I could see that. Unfortunately, we weren't getting anywhere very fast. None of this would be of interest to Felix. He would know it all anyway.

I tried to tease other stuff out of her, like what the brothers did when they were off duty. Where did they go? What about families? Did they have cars, planes, boats? Did they go fishing? Stuff like that. But it was no good. She didn't seem to know very much at all.

It was no good, that is, until she stopped and suddenly looked thoughtful. I stared at her, my eyebrows raised in hope.

'Make some more coffee, will you, Frank?' she said with a frown. 'Something's coming loose in there, but it needs heavy-duty caffeine to encourage it.'

I jumped to it. If Lady felt more coffee would help, I was just the man to provide it.

* * *

'Transportation,' she said slowly, savouring the word as she stirred her coffee. 'It was when you talked about cars and things that something came to mind. I don't know if it's relevant or not, though.' She looked at me for guidance.

'Just spill it out,' I told her. 'Like I said, we're brainstorming here. Who can tell if something's relevant or not before we look at it?'

'The brothers have one of those superyachts. You know what I mean? The great big, mega things that can sail the seven seas, and are big enough to not mind bumping into icebergs?'

I nodded. 'I know what you mean. There used to be one around here several years ago. That was owned by a Russian, too.'

'They like big and fancy, those guys. That's for sure.'

'What do the brothers do with their superyacht?' I asked. 'Where does it live?'

'It comes and goes a lot, from the way Georgi used to talk about it. I've only seen it the once myself, and that was from a distance, but Georgi was often on it. He used to enjoy trying to make me jealous.'

'Where does it go when it comes into Chicago?'

'It just stays in the boatyard.'

'What boatyard?'

She looked puzzled. 'Their boatyard!'

'Oh, I see. Their boatyard.'

Wheels began to spin inside my head, as I took in the enormity of what she was telling me and started fitting pieces together that until now had seemed unconnected.

Her face lightened as she thought about it with evident amusement. 'Georgi said he would take me with him some day on one of their trips.'

With a sigh, she added, 'That won't happen now, though.'

'No,' I admitted. 'Probably not.'

'I'd like to have seen it. Georgi said it has its own helicopters. Even a miniature submarine that can dock inside the yacht! Can you imagine that?'

'Not easily.'

'Anyway, it's no great loss, I guess. I might not have come back from any trip Georgi took me on.'

I changed the subject.

'This may be it,' I told her quietly, hardly daring to believe it.

CHAPTER FORTY

'Drugs,' I said. 'Drugs. One brother in South America. Their own superyacht — with onboard helicopter and submarine — that docks in their own boatyard at the bottom end of Lake Michigan, just outside Chicago. Wow!'

Lady stared at me and said thoughtfully, 'I never put it all together like that. It might be something.'

'It certainly might!'

Whether it gave us something to offer Felix, though, I wasn't sure. But it was worth thinking about. The Miskovs were probably running the importation of illicit drugs on an industrial scale, and bringing the stuff right into the heart of a major metropolis. Putting them out of business would be a major strike for US law enforcement agencies — and national security.

My initial excitement dimmed a bit as I thought more about it. The trouble was twofold. One, how likely was it that the US authorities didn't already know something of it? Not very, probably.

Two, what would we be offering Felix? Just a suggestion, really. Advice that they should look into the possibility. It was a bit thin, when you thought about it. They could just take it and do nothing in return. Lady would be no better off.

'I don't think it will fly, unfortunately,' I said with a reluctant sigh. 'We'll have to come up with something else, something better.'

* * *

It was late. We were out of ideas. We were tired. It was time to get some sleep.

We settled down quietly in the bunk beds again, each of us with our own thoughts. For my part, I continued wrestling with the problem of what we could offer Felix that might entice him to bite. Suggestions, hints and ideas wouldn't be anywhere near enough. He would just laugh. It had to be something concrete, something firm.

Maybe something staged, as well. If it was a one-off, he could take it and then renege on the deal, and laugh at us. We had to come up with something that was in parts. Offer him a bit of something that he could assess and that would make him come back for more, and keep that going while Lady got away somewhere.

Where, though? That was something else we hadn't discussed yet. But we should. We needed some sort of idea about where she could go, and how long it would take her to get there.

'Are you awake?' I whispered.

'Yes. Of course I am.'

'I'm just thinking. Where would you go? If you could get away from here, where would you head for? Somewhere in the US?'

'I don't know. Probably. Perhaps not, though. Somewhere without extradition would be better, I suppose. But I just haven't thought about it.'

'I guess it might depend on whether they gave you a full and permanent release, or just a five-minute interval while they looked the other way.'

'You got that right!' she said with a sigh. 'That would make a big difference.'

I grimaced. There was more to this than I'd first thought. No easy answers, either.

'Well, we'll just have to see how it goes.' I stretched, yawned and added, 'I'm going to shut down now. I need to be up early, to go and see if I've still got a cottage up there on the cliff top.'

'Lucas and his boys are going to pay if anything has happened to it,' Lady said briskly. 'I can promise you that!'

I smiled. I believed she meant it, really meant it.

* * *

Despite the situation, I had no trouble getting to sleep. I rarely do. Especially in the hut. I wouldn't say it's peaceful there, or quiet. Not at all. But most of the sounds are generated by the natural world, and that makes a difference. The sea can be rough and noisy, or gentle and persistent. The gulls squabble wildly at times, and call plaintively at others. There are foghorns to be heard some nights, but even they seem to be more natural than man-made. And it's usually dark-sky dark, which helps. So, for me, it's not a threatening environment, down there in the hut. It's a very comfortable place to be.

So I went to sleep quickly and didn't wake up until Lady said, 'Frank, are you awake?'

My eyes opened instantly, my brain having been summoned from the depths.

'I am now,' I grumbled. 'What time is it?'

'Six thirty. Sorry if it's too early for you. It's just that I've thought of something I should have mentioned.'

I turned on to my back with a sigh, staring at the base of the upper bunk. 'What?'

'Encryption,' she said.

CHAPTER FORTY-ONE

'Encryption?'

'You know what it is, Frank, don't you?'

'Coding. Coded messages, so the uninitiated can't read them.'

'That's right.'

I yawned. 'So what the hell has that got to do with anything?'

'Sorry I woke you. It's probably too early for you.'

You're right! I thought, peering around through the darkness, although it wasn't really dark. Not black, anyway. Luminescence from the sea saw to that. All the same, it wasn't light enough, morning enough, to have me jumping out of my warm sleeping bag.

'What do you want to talk about?' I asked instead, making an effort.

'You know about encrypted messages flying around the internet — emails, WhatsApp, and so on?'

'What about them?'

'They bug the hell out of the cops and the authorities,' she said with a chuckle. 'Facebook, WhatsApp and the software companies won't let 'em know how to read them either.'

'So I understand.' *For God's sake!* I felt like screaming. *Just let me get back to sleep, please.*

'The Miskov brothers use encryption when they're dealing with the Russians.'

'Why am I not surprised?' I said, yawning again. 'The Russians probably insist on it.'

There was a long gap then, in which nothing more was said. I began to drift off, heading back into the realm of sleep.

'I know the encryption password they use,' Lady said quietly.

For a moment or two nothing happened. Then I jerked upright, banging my head on a corner post.

'What?' I gasped, grimacing with pain, and sure I must have misheard.

Lady laughed. 'I thought that might wake you up!'

'So you just said it to wake me up, did you?'

'Nope. I meant it.'

That did it. I got out of my sleeping bag and straightened up, ready now to start the day.

'Really?' I said.

'Yep.'

'Let's go, then!'

Even though I couldn't see her face, I could tell she was smiling. If what she'd said was true, she had something to smile about — quite apart from having made me get up first.

I switched on a battery lamp. Then I picked up the kettle, poured water into it and lit the little camping stove. I placed the kettle on the stove and sat down on one of the two wooden kitchen chairs that lived in the hut.

'Tell me more,' I ordered.

CHAPTER FORTY-TWO

What Lady had to say was simple and straightforward. She had witnessed Georgi sending and receiving messages once or twice, and just happened to have memorized the password he had used. She hadn't set out to do that. It had just lodged itself in her memory.

'And that's the code they use with the Russians?'

She shook her head. 'Not only with them. They use it for all communication at a senior level in the organization, as well as with the Russians.'

I pondered what she had just said for a moment, while I made a couple of mugs of coffee. It sounded too good to be true, which reminded me of the old saying — if it sounds, or looks, too good to be true, then it probably is.

'We haven't got much for breakfast,' I said, playing for time while I thought things through. 'Just bread and cheese.'

'I don't eat breakfast.' She lowered herself from the heady height up top. 'Coffee is fine.'

I pushed one of the mugs across the table to her.

'You must have a pretty good memory,' I suggested, 'to have remembered the code.'

'I suppose I do. It goes with the territory.'

'What territory is that?' I asked, thinking *hitman country*.

'As a musician, a singer. All singers have good memories. Without one, they couldn't do their job.'

'I'd never thought of that,' I admitted, looking at her with surprise.

It was true. I hadn't. It had never occurred to me that a singer needs a good memory. Nor had it really sunk in that Lady was more than an apprentice hitman.

'So you're a singer — not just a bathtub yodeller?'

She grinned and nodded. 'Yep, I am. I sing in clubs, places like that. That was where Boris, the older Miskov brother, first saw me, and took a shine to me. In case you're wondering,' she added, 'that club was where Felix had planted me, so that Boris would see me.'

I kept away from the question of how, in detail, that had worked out. I could guess.

'Blues?'

She nodded. 'Oh, yes. I never really had a choice about that. My dad brought me up to be a blues vocalist. Gave me the name, and so on.'

'Even though blues is traditionally black music?'

'And . . . what? You think I'm white?'

'Well . . . Yes, actually.'

'My mom was white, apparently, but Dad was black. And he just loved Billie Holiday.'

'I see,' I said slowly, trying to cover my confusion.

Mixed race, eh? But, yes, I had assumed she was white. That was what she looked. Californian white, perhaps, with a lovely light tan. She was a bonny woman.

'The genes have a mind of their own,' she said with a chuckle. 'Don't worry about it, Frank. I don't.'

I gave her a rueful smile and said, 'So that's what you do in your spare time — sing blues?'

'Yep. The colour of your skin, or your parents, doesn't matter at all if you can sing worth a damn.'

'As it should be.'

'Right. Anyway, blues ain't just black music. Think Van Morrison, Van the Man.'

I shrugged, acknowledging my ignorance of the genre.

'Are you any good?'

'What at? Singing?'

I nodded.

'Some.' She shrugged and added, 'But I followed the money, and went where the money was better.'

I didn't know if she was talking about gangs, drugs or just killing people. It seemed safer to change the subject.

'Going back to the memory question,' I said, 'and just out of curiosity, how many songs do you actually know — well enough to be able to sing them, I mean?'

She shrugged again. 'Maybe a hundred. Something like that, I suppose. I don't really know. I've never counted them.'

Wow! How come it had never occurred to me that singers needed not just good memories but great memories?

'So when you heard Georgi reciting the password on the phone, you had no trouble remembering it?'

'He didn't do that. Georgi couldn't remember shit! He had it written down on a bit of paper. He wasn't supposed to, but he did, and I saw it. That's all,' she added, with a shrug. 'I didn't set out to remember it, but it found a place in my memory bank just the same.'

'Was it an easy word to remember?'

She shook her head. 'Not a word. Just a string of letters and numbers.'

And she had remembered them!

'Glory be!' I breathed, still scarcely able to believe it. 'If you're right, and it's true, this changes everything. Now we have something Felix will be prepared to die for.'

CHAPTER FORTY-THREE

In a preliminary way, we ran through how it could work out, if things went well. It was obvious there was going to be a lot to do. Time to roll up our sleeves and get on with it. Not from here, though. We couldn't do anything from the hut.

When we climbed back up the cliff it was an enormous relief to me that both the cottages were still standing. For one thing, it meant I didn't have to face Jimmy Mack and tell him what had happened in his absence.

Standing right next to my cottage was a police vehicle in standard garish livery. No doubt it had had something to do with the cottages surviving the night. I gave Lady the key to my front door and went to have a word with the officer sitting behind the wheel. Luckily the cottage had obscured his view of us appearing over the cliff edge.

'Frank Doy,' I told him, holding out my driving licence for ID. 'Been any trouble?'

'Not while I've been here.' He gave the document a brief glance. Then he grinned and added, 'Where did you come from? I was wondering who you were. I was just about ready to call for reinforcements!'

'We just walked back,' I told him. 'Been here long?'

'An hour or so. I took over from another officer. We've been keeping an eye on the place overnight.'

'Thanks. I'm very glad you have — and very grateful. I couldn't risk staying here last night. Now we'll have to see what the new day brings. Will you have a cup of coffee?'

He shook his head. 'No, thanks. I need to be on my way now you're back. I'll just report in first.'

I thanked him again and left him to it. I walked back to the cottage, and the open front door. Lady had anticipated me, and had already got the kettle on.

'Everything all right?' she asked anxiously.

'Seems to be. They've been keeping watch overnight. That officer said nothing had happened while he's been here. I'll find out from Bill Peart what happened when the police arrived last night. I'll ring him now, and tell him we don't need him anymore.'

'Don't we?'

I shook my head. 'I have a better idea.'

* * *

'Pandemonium,' Bill said, when I asked him what had happened. 'Absolute bloody pandemonium!'

I winced.

'It looked like an invasion force had arrived,' he said with satisfaction. 'Men everywhere around your property — and Mr Mack's.'

Even more reason to grimace.

'So how was it handled?'

'By sheer good luck, our helicopter was available. They got there first, and floodlit the scene from above. They broadcast warnings when they saw what was happening, or about to happen.'

'And then?'

'And then the invasion force scattered. Took off in their three vehicles before our ground patrols arrived. The pilot followed one of them for a time, but was running short of fuel and had to break off the pursuit over Middlesbrough.'

'So there was no direct contact?'

'No.'

Thank God for that, I couldn't help thinking. Even if the police responders had included firearms officers, it could have turned out nasty. I should have warned Bill. But then there would have been delay, and the cottages would have been trashed and probably burned to the ground. So things had worked out fine. We'd all been lucky.

'Well, thanks for all that, Bill. They'll not be back now they know you're involved.'

'You sure about that?'

'I'm sure.'

'Just as well. We've got our work cut out, as it is, looking for these characters. But let me know if there's any further sign of them.'

'Of course.'

'Done?' Lady asked, after I switched off the phone.

I nodded. 'Done — for now. But I'll have to be more open with him at some point soon. After you've gone,' I added with a wry smile.

'Good.'

'Now let's eat,' I suggested, grateful that I'd nipped to the shop while taking Lady to hospital.

* * *

We sat at the kitchen table with our coffee and a hastily scrambled-together meal of eggs and toast, which went down very well in my case.

'You must be hungry,' Lady said, picking at what was on her plate.

'Starving. You?'

She shook her head. 'Breakfast,' she said, with a disdainful sniff.

It was up to her, but I needed to eat.

'Right,' I said, when I was finished, 'let's talk more business now. There's a lot to do.'

'How do you want to play this?'

'First, I think you should contact Felix. Let him know you're still alive, despite Lucas's appearance on the scene. And then tell him you want to meet. There are things you're not prepared to talk about over the phone.'

'No way! I'm not going to meet him,' she said, shaking her head violently. 'He won't be on his own. I wouldn't get away alive.'

'It's all right, it's all right!' I assured her. 'It will be me, not you, that actually meets him. I just want you to set it up. It's no good me asking to meet. He'd just hang up the phone on me.'

Lady agreed. 'You're right. He knows about Georgi. So, as far as he's concerned, the operation is over. He'll just want to clear up loose ends — me, in other words — and get the hell out. Contain the damage.'

'My thoughts, exactly. So he'll be eager to meet you, preferably somewhere isolated. The more isolated the better, as far as he's concerned. So here's what I suggest . . .'

* * *

My proposed venue for a meeting was the big, open car park in Coatham where Georgi had met his end, and I had so nearly met mine. Lady could tell Felix that she wanted to show him where it had all gone wrong. It made sense. She was desperate. She wanted to make him see that she had had no choice, and hope that he understood and agreed.

Felix would, of course. He would both understand and agree, but it would make no difference. The operation was over. The only way he could make sure the negative fallout was contained was if Lady did not walk away from the scene. Taking her away and returning her to prison was not an option. Back there, in the federal penitentiary system, she would continue to be a risk to him and to those for whom he worked. She would have to be eliminated to avert that.

Besides, Lady's death could bring about a neat closure here, too. The local cops would no longer have an unsolved murder case on their hands if things went well. They wouldn't need to continue looking for the killer. To the middle-management mind, a mind such as Felix's undoubtedly was, there was a certain logic and satisfaction to be found in that scenario.

* * *

To round preparations off, I phoned Leon. It was time, high time, to take up his offer. We needed help, help of the kind that Cleveland Police couldn't be asked to provide, and weren't really capable of providing anyway.

Then I went out and did a bit of clearing up outside. It wasn't necessary, but I needed to think about something else for a few minutes. I needed a break. It was all a bit too intense.

One thing I was grateful for was Jimmy Mack's absence. He was away convalescing, having had a hip replacement, at his sister's place in Whitby. I was glad he wasn't here, both for his own security and for my peace of mind. It was one thing less to worry about. I would have been run ragged trying to cope with both him and Lady Day.

CHAPTER FORTY-FOUR

There were a few cars lined up facing the sea, against the edge of the car park. Possibly one or two had someone in them, but I didn't think so. Mostly they would have been driven here by dog owners once again, who were now walking on the beach.

I headed for the SUV standing alone in the middle of the vast expanse of tarmac. As I drew up, just a few yards away, a man got out. As far as I could see, there was no one else in the vehicle. But I didn't believe he would have come alone. Somewhere in the vicinity there would be support for him.

I parked so that my door was facing the driver's door of the other vehicle, and got out slowly.

'Mr Felix?'

The man watching me closely didn't respond immediately. He just stared at me with a forbidding, unfriendly look. I stood beside my car and spoke to him in what I hoped he would think a non-threatening voice.

'I represent Lady Day,' I said quietly. 'She has asked me to meet you on her behalf, and to put certain things to you. I would very much appreciate it if you would hear me out.'

He was a lean, tough-looking guy, snappily dressed in expensive if casual outdoor clothes. About fortyish, I guessed.

And a control freak. His demeanour was one of calm confidence, which I could see would be intimidating if you weren't sure of yourself or had anything to fear.

'I don't know who or what you're talking about,' he said crisply in a cultivated American accent. 'Who did you say you are?'

'I didn't. But the name is Frank Doy. I live locally, and Ms Day retained me to represent her.'

'You're a lawyer?'

'Not actually.' I shook my head. 'I'm all sorts of things, but definitely not a lawyer. More of a professional negotiator, I would say.'

Nothing changed. He hadn't got back in his vehicle and driven away. His expression hadn't changed. He still looked at me as if I was something on the sole of his shoe.

I didn't mind that. I wasn't impressed. Plenty of more dangerous men than him had tried their psychological warfare on me.

'Ms Day arranged to meet you here,' I continued. 'Presumably you agree that that's true?'

He said nothing.

'Having thought it over, she decided it would be better if I came instead of her. Essentially, she wants me to offer you a deal. That's why I'm here.'

He chuckled and appeared amused now. 'A deal? What kind of deal would that be?'

I maintained my gravity and my legalistic delivery. That seemed to work best in negotiations. Keep it cool. Keep it unemotional. Stick to the facts. Let the other guy do anger, frustration, or whatever.

'You're aware, I believe, that things got out of hand here the other day. Ms Day's boss sadly died when he tried to kill her. In the circumstances, she has decided she must abandon the arrangement she has with you. In return for you not trying to stop her walking away, she will give you information about the Miskov brothers' business operations that she believes you will find of great value.'

'Is that so?' he said with sarcastic venom.

'It is, yes.'

Smiling with even greater confidence, and perhaps even more amusement now he knew what this was about, he said, 'You do realize, Mr Doy, that you've put your life on the line, coming here like this?'

'No more than you have. And we're not equally exposed. This is my home ground. But it's a long way from home for you.'

We stared at each other for a long moment then.

But my confident words had done it. He'd lost control of the moment, and he knew it.

What have you got?' he snapped savagely. 'What has she given you?'

We began to talk business then.

'For a start,' I said, 'we can provide a lot of detail concerning the Miskovs and their organization — properties, people, addresses, activities . . .'

'Don't waste my time,' he snapped.

He obviously believed they already had all that.

'Not good enough, eh? Well, OK. Here's something else, something you might not know.'

'It had better be good.'

'The brothers own what we over here on this side of the Atlantic call a superyacht. They also have a boatyard, where the superyacht docks when it comes home from its frequent sailings. How convenient that must be for their import trade in illegal drugs, eh?

'And here's something else. As well as helicopters, the superyacht carries a little submarine deep in its intestines. Guess what that adds up to!'

'A narco-sub,' he said, nodding. 'We'll have it checked out.'

'And another thing for you to check out while you're at it. Lady thought the Miskovs are building a bigger submarine in that boatyard of theirs. They're planning to scale things up.'

‘Probably,’ he admitted.

‘How am I doing so far? More to the point, how is Lady doing?’

‘I’ll be frank with you. This is all of some interest, and some of it is even new to me. I admit that. But it’s nowhere near enough for me to allow her to just walk away, if that’s what she’s hoping. This is information she should be providing anyway. It’s why we set her up. Is that all you have?’

‘So it’s not going to get her released?’

He shook his head.

‘How about you just look the other way while she makes herself scarce?’

He grinned, as if that was the funniest thing he’d ever heard.

‘No good, huh?’

‘Look, pal. Just tell her to get herself back here pronto, or it will be the worse for her.’

Worse? Worse than what was on offer already? Worse than being returned to high-max prison — or summary execution, which seemed more likely? I didn’t think so.

He turned away, the meeting seemingly over as far as he was concerned.

‘There is one other thing that might be of interest to you, and might change your mind.’

‘I doubt it. I doubt that very much,’ he said over his shoulder, as he headed back to his car.

But I didn’t. I didn’t doubt it at all. It was where I’d been leading all along. Lady had given me the ace of spades.

‘Lady Day knows the encryption key the top Miskov people use for all their electronic communications, including those with Russian intelligence operatives in the United States.’

He stopped. Slowly, he turned round and stared at me.

‘Just think about it,’ I said, getting back into my car. ‘And think about what you could offer her in exchange for that information. We’ll wait to hear from you.’

CHAPTER FORTY-FIVE

As I drove away, I wasn't in any doubt that Felix was hooked. He would want that key very much indeed. Already his brain would be bulging with thought of the possibilities it could provide. Now we'd have to wait and see what he came up with in exchange for it. Whatever he proposed ought to be a hell of a lot better than his response to the other stuff I'd given him.

* * *

Back at Risky Point, I found Lady outside, talking to Jimmy Mack. I grimaced at the sight. It was a great pity Jimmy's sister hadn't detained him longer. I just hoped he hadn't come home too soon. I didn't want him to find himself in the middle of a gun battle with Lucas's mob, or with Felix's crew, come to that.

That thought reminded me that there was no reason now to hide anything I knew about Lucas and his gang from the police. Lady was done with Lucas and the Miskov brothers, and Felix knew that. Equally, I was done with them, now I knew who had put the contract on my head, and that it was all to do with their search for Sasha.

So there was no reason at all for me to hold back any longer. No further need for secrecy. I had all the information I needed. I could set Bill Peart on them. *At last!* he would no doubt say.

'This young lady says she's from America,' Jimmy said.

'That's right. Has she introduced herself to you?'

Jimmy smiled. 'Lady, she says she's called. Lady Day. Isn't that a beautiful name?'

'Yes, it is.'

'She's broke her arm, she says. But it's getting better now. She can move it, and use it a bit.'

'Well, good to know!' I responded, wondering what else she had told him. Pretty much everything, it sounded like. Jimmy had a way with young women. He must have been a right lad in his youth.

'It was nice meeting you, Jimmy,' Lady said. 'I'm going inside now, but I'll see you again, I hope?'

'Most certainly,' Jimmy told her with a beaming smile. 'I'll have to tell you more about the fishing.'

'I'll look forward to that, Jimmy.'

She turned to walk away, and Jimmy's eyes followed her. I'm sure he would have taken his hat off to her, had he been wearing one.

* * *

Back indoors, I asked her if her arm really was feeling better.

'A bit. Anyway, I need to start using it again.'

'Just don't overdo it,' I said, closing the door behind us.

'How did it go?' she demanded then, swinging round on me.

'Pretty good, I think.'

'Did he bite?'

'We'll have to see about that, but I think so. He's definitely interested in the encryption angle. I went through the other stuff with him first, but he wasn't interested. Even if he hadn't known some of it, once I told him he had it — for free. He didn't need to offer you anything.

'So I played our trump card, and that stopped him in his tracks. I told him you knew the key, and we wanted him to think about what he's prepared to offer for it.'

'How did he respond?'

'I didn't give him the chance. I just told him to think about it and get in touch if he's interested.'

She looked thoughtful for a moment. 'He can call. He's got the number.'

'Yeah. Well, we'll just have to see. But, remember, we don't give him anything more until he makes an offer that's acceptable. You need to be able to walk away from here without having to look over your shoulder for ever more.'

'I'm used to doing that.'

'Even so. There's a chance now of changing your life, and making all that unnecessary.'

I really hoped something could be worked out. The encryption key would be a treasure chest for Felix. There was no doubt about that. With it, he could bring down the Miskovs, and perhaps do more than that. He might even be able to round up a pile of Russian agents and operatives in the United States, and thereby do a lot to improve national security. Mind-boggling for a career security agent.

Yet what I was in doubt about was whether the key would truly buy Lady her freedom, which was what it was all about for us. After all, Felix could say yes. Then we could make a deal and hand over the code. But what if he changed his mind or was overruled by someone higher up in the hierarchy?

Realistically, what could we do about that? Agreements reached in the shadows of the intelligence world would cut little ice on Capitol Hill, or wherever it is that American politicos and lawyers deal with national security issues.

The more I thought about it, the more it became blindingly obvious that once Lady handed over the key, we had no way of stopping them from ignoring a deal, short of holding Felix hostage until she got clear. I didn't want to be party to anything like that, not least because then I could find myself on the CIA elimination list, as a potential witness to their illegal activities. That would be even worse than having the Miskov brothers' contract hanging over me.

Nor could I see Felix allowing Lady to go anywhere until he got the password from her. He would distrust her quite as much as she distrusted him. I was sure of that.

Logjam, then! Stalemate. What to do?

On reflection, an outlandish possibility that might be worth exploring came to mind. I decided to phone Henry about it when I had a moment.

* * *

Meanwhile, there was something else that needed doing. First, though, I wanted to let Lady know.

'By the way,' I said, 'I'm going to let the police know more about Lucas and his pals. Who they are. Where they're based. Where you and Georgi were staying. All that.'

'You can't!' she said, horrified.

I knew that for her it meant crossing a line people in her world didn't cross unless they had a death wish, or were feeling absolutely desperate or vindictive. It seemed to me that this was pretty close to one of those times.

'Think about it,' I suggested. 'You're out of it now, but Lucas and his pals are going to keep on coming unless something stops them. That's got to be either the cops or Leon's people. And, frankly, I would rather it was the police than Leon's people. I don't want a pile of dead bodies on my doorstep.'

Put like that, she could see what good sense it would make for me to call Bill Peart once again.

CHAPTER FORTY-SIX

Lady looked at me anxiously when the phone buzzed. I glanced at the number and smiled to encourage her. 'Let's see, shall we?'

I let it buzz some more before I picked it up.

'Yes?'

'Frank Doy?'

Felix.

'That's me. How can I help?'

'I'll not mess you about, Frank. We want the encryption key you mentioned. How much do you want for it?'

Inwardly, I breathed a sigh of relief. I like a man who comes straight to the point. I always feel you can do business with someone like that.

'In return for the password, Lady Day goes free. That's the price. No money involved. Just let her go.'

'Can't be done,' he said crisply. 'Cash on the table is the offer.'

'We're not interested, in that case. Either she walks, or you don't get the key.'

'I don't think you understand, Frank. I can't overturn the law and a judge's verdict. My bosses can't either. That's just how it is. Fact of life.'

'Good day to you, then. You know the price. Contact me if you change your mind.'

'So he wouldn't budge?' Lady said, looking dispirited.

'Not yet,' I said with a shrug. 'We need to be patient. He'll be back.'

'You sound like a negotiator!' she said bitterly. 'What I need is a salesman.'

'That's exactly what I am, a negotiator. No other word for it. Let's just leave it with him for now.'

'Maybe he's not that bothered about the fucking key!' she said bitterly.

'Oh, he is! Don't you worry about that. He wants it very badly indeed. Legal process is the stumbling block. Let's just wait and see if he can find a way through it.

'If he can't,' I added with a grin, 'and he comes for you anyway, Leon's men will take care of him, as well as Lucas.'

CHAPTER FORTY-SEVEN

'Something's going on,' Bill growled when I phoned him. 'And you're right in the middle of it — and not telling me!'

I grimaced. Then I said, 'Well, I can tell you this much. I now know where the gang that have been creating so much trouble are based.' I read out the address that Lady had given me. 'It's a former farmhouse, now a holiday let, in a village not far from Stokesley. They've leased it.'

'And you know this how?'

'From a tip-off, Bill. I believe it's genuine.'

'We'll check it out.'

'Be careful! These guys play rough, and they're armed.'

He chewed it over for a moment and then said, 'This had better be good, Frank. I'm under pressure.'

'Pressure?'

I was about to laugh and say he wouldn't know what pressure was until he had a contract on his head and a gun pointed in his face, but wisely, I desisted.

'Yes, pressure. I'm getting a lot of hassle from upstairs.'

The upper echelons of the force, he meant. So he wasn't in the mood for jokes. I was going to have to help him out some more, if our beautiful friendship was to be preserved.

CHAPTER FORTY-EIGHT

Next, I phoned Henry, my go-to guy when I need some research or number-crunching done.

'What?' he said.

'You usually say "What now?" when my number comes up. How the heck are you, Henry?'

'Broke. You?'

'About the same.'

'You're no good to me, then.'

He broke off to do some coughing. An unrepentant smoker of long standing, Henry did a lot of coughing. I waited till he had finished.

'Can you do some urgent research for me?'

'Only if it pays well.'

'Henry, I always pay — and I always pay what you ask.'

'True, I suppose,' he said grudgingly. 'So what do you want?'

'I want to know if it's possible in America to be given a pardon for a capital crime for which you've been convicted and are serving a life sentence in prison. Also, if it is possible, how do you go about getting one?'

Henry didn't seem surprised by my request, nor perturbed. He liked anything out of the ordinary, and I often presented him with a challenge. I may even have been his favourite client for that reason.

'Urgent? Does that mean you have someone in mind?'

'Yes, I do. She's on the run and staying with me. I'm hoping to keep her safe.'

'Ah!'

It wasn't much of a comment, but it was enough. Henry understood.

'I'll get right on it,' he added.

CHAPTER FORTY-NINE

I stood on the cliff top watching a distant helicopter heading in towards the coast. They're not my favourite mode of transportation, those things. I admit they can be useful, very useful even, but if something happens to the engine, they fall out of the sky. Not like an autumn leaf drifting pleasantly in the breeze, as a small, fixed-wing plane might do. They just drop like a big rock plunging into the sea from the cliff top. No chance to get out. Then they sink, fast. The best thing to do is not to get on board in the first place.

Still, this one was going steadily enough, with no hint of engine trouble. What was more, it was heading this way. It was going to pass over the coastline very close to Risky Point, and I thought it might well be using our cliff as a navigation aid. I wondered if it was a rescue craft that had flown up the coast from Flamborough Head. They often do, before turning inland. It's a well-followed route for training purposes.

This one didn't do that. Instead of heading inland, it slowed as it reached the coast and began to manoeuvre over Risky Point. I winced at the noise as it circled overhead for a couple of minutes. Then it began to descend. By then, I was worried. I was hoping I hadn't got it wrong and that this wasn't a CIA intervention ordered by Felix, come to abduct Lady Day.

The chopper hovered about thirty feet overhead. A rope was flung out of the open doorway, and several figures used it to slide fast to the ground. Shit! I'd been caught flat-footed, daydreaming. What the hell was I going to do now, I thought desperately, as the figures spread out fast in all directions, securing a perimeter.

And where the hell was Lady? I spun round, trying frantically to think of something to do to help her.

Then the chopper came all the way down to rest on the ground, at which point Leon Podolsky appeared in the doorway and jumped down. He strode towards me with a big grin on his stupid face.

Incredulous, all I could do for a moment was shake my head. Then I started to laugh, with relief as much as anything. This was just so typical of a Podolsky operation. Leon loved to create drama.

'Good to see you!' I shouted, struggling to make myself heard over the noise from the chopper.

'I've brought you some help, Frank,' he shouted back. 'It sounded like you need it.'

'I certainly do!'

We shook hands, and then he grabbed me in his trademark bear hug.

'I've brought a few of my men,' he said as he stepped back. 'Good men. They know what to do, how to handle things.'

I nodded, still taking in what was happening.

'They won't bother you,' he added. 'They're self-contained and self-sufficient. You won't even know they're here, until or unless you need them.'

'Thanks, Leon. I actually hope I won't need them, but how do I get in touch with them if I do?'

'Just use this,' he said, handing me a small, slim phone. 'It's set to contact Dmitri, the commander, immediately. Likewise, he can contact you. Keep it on at all times.'

'I'd like to meet him.'

'Of course. Let him sort out his men first. Then he will come to see you.'

'Will they stay in the cottage?' I asked, wondering how I was going to accommodate so many extra bodies.

He shook his head. 'These are field troops, Frank. They're used to looking after themselves, often in pretty hostile environments. They're happier outdoors. That's better for them, and for you.'

I let it go. Leon was from a tough school. The people he employed were, too. They would be ex-Spetsnaz, like him. Perhaps not so ex- at all. Leon had been moving in pretty exalted circles since I first met him, and no doubt he could call on resources to match his new status.

Once, he had been a pariah as far as dominant circles in the Kremlin were concerned, but times had changed. A less hostile group, or *kvorst*, had won the ear of the president, and Leon had made peace by agreeing to serve for a time as governor in a region of Russia's Far East. Who knew what he was now? I had no idea, but I was confident he was still the man I knew.

'Come on inside,' I told him. 'It's too noisy out here.'

'Thank you, but I must warn you I can't stay long.'

As I recalled, he never did stay anywhere long. Being busy was one reason. Continually making himself a moving target for reasons of personal security was another, one I had always thought even more important. His arrival here at Risky Point had been overwhelming, as his appearances so often in the past had been, but I was beginning to recover.

He turned to beckon to a figure who had stayed close to the helicopter. The figure started walking swiftly towards us.

'Yes,' Leon said with a smile, seeing rather than hearing my gasp of surprise. 'I've also brought someone you know.'

By then, I had identified the approaching figure. I turned and held out my arms in welcome.

CHAPTER FIFTY

Henry got back to me pretty quickly, as he usually does.

'If we're talking federal crime and federal prison,' he said without preamble, 'it's very difficult. It would require the president to pardon her. State crime and state prison, it's down to the governor of the state in question.'

'This is federal. So it can be done?'

'Difficult, but not impossible. Federal or state, it needs effective lobbying. So you need somebody with clout to bat for you in the Oval Office in this case.'

'But federal pardons are actually possible?'

'Yeah. I got some stats. Generally, the numbers of pardons and commutations, as they call them, have gone up over the past century, but every year, under every president, there have always been some.

'I would need more time to look deeper for patterns, but the numbers reflect things like how many submissions were made, whether the country was at war or not, how long a president had been in office, and so on.'

'And, presumably, a president's political leanings?'

'Well, maybe. But that's not straightforward. Jimmy Carter pardoned 534 people in his one term in office, while Trump only pardoned 28. So you might think you can see the conservative bias there. Or a religious bias, Carter being a God-fearing, Christian sort of bloke.

'On the other hand, Obama pardoned 212 and Nixon 863. No correlation at all with political leanings there. Quite the reverse, in fact. The leftie comes out quite draconian, compared with Attila the Hun — so to speak.

'The biggest pardoner of them all was President Truman, with 1,913. Nobody else has even come close to that score. Maybe he was on a guilt trip for dropping atomic bombs on Japan.'

The recitation of statistics was making my eyes water, but it served a purpose, and it gave me hope.

'What you're saying, Henry, is that, however difficult, pardons really are possible?'

'Definitely. Tell your lady friend not to give up hope.'

My feeling, exactly.

'Any idea how to go about trying to get a pardon?'

'Well, you need a petition, probably presented by a lawyer. That has to go to the office of the Pardon Attorney. But, like I said before, you really need a big hitter on your side, one with access to the president's ear.'

'Thanks, Henry.'

CHAPTER FIFTY-ONE

'Sasha!'

'Hi, Frank!' She wore a big grin as she came to meet me. 'How are you? In trouble over me again?'

'You could say that,' I admitted, laughing and giving her another hug.

'I thought it might help to have her here,' Leon said, 'as this seems to be all about Sasha.'

'My plan was to keep her out of it, Leon, but this is still a very welcome surprise. How are you, Sasha?'

'Alive still, and much the same. Now, what's all this about?'

'Come on inside! It's too noisy to talk out here.'

I steered my visitors towards the cottage.

* * *

Their arrival was overwhelming, so unexpected had it been, but I was recovering by the time we got inside, where Lady was waiting to meet us. I assumed that she had been even more astonished by this development, and hurried to reassure her.

'These are my old Russian friends,' I told her. 'They've come to help us. Leon and Sasha, please meet Lady Day.'

It was a tricky moment. They all looked at each other and nodded. Then Leon held out his hand and Lady shook it, which was a good start.

With the two women, it was a bit different. They both knew something about the other's part in this play they were joining, but as they eyed each other, I sensed that each was wondering about the other's connection to me. I decided to speed things up.

'Sasha, Lady was being used by a Chicago criminal gang, commissioned by Red Star, to try to find you through me. She was brought out of a federal prison in the United States and placed with the gang by the CIA, in order to help them bring down the Chicago mobsters and disrupt Red Star operations in America.

'Here, she shot and killed her boss, the favourite son of the head man, who tried to kill her. That meant she had signed her own death warrant with the gang, and possibly also with the CIA. If she was lucky, she would be returned to prison, which she was determined to avoid. Unlucky, and she would never even reach the prison.'

'That was when I became involved. I tried to help her. It suited us both to work together. Lady wanted to survive. And I wanted to find you, Sasha, to warn you that you were being hunted. But we've been outnumbered and struggling all along. So I turned to my old friend Leon for help.

'And here we all are,' I concluded, with a shrug and a wry smile. 'Now, please sit down, all of you. Let's have a coffee or a beer, and talk about what we're going to do.'

* * *

After we were done, Leon took my arm and said, 'I need to leave in a few minutes, Frank, but first let us step outside and get some fresh air. I need to tell you about my daughters, and how things are in Prague these days.'

We left the two women in the cottage and walked over to the edge of the cliff. Leon gazed out at the sea as if he had never seen it before. 'So majestic,' he said quietly. 'I envy you living in such a place, Frank.'

I smiled. 'It wouldn't suit you, Leon. Far too quiet — usually!'

He laughed.

'So how are Olga and Lenka?'

'Very well, thank you. Nothing has changed with them.'

That was all he said about Olga and Lenka. He said nothing at all about Prague. Nor about his wife and son in Switzerland. But, then, he never had said much about them. They were his secret, and kept safe by being kept secret.

Looking directly at me, he said, 'I have heard from my contacts in Chicago, Frank. Am I to assume you know who, and what, Lady Day is?'

'I think I do, Leon.'

'A contract killer?'

I nodded. 'Also a blues singer, I believe.'

He smiled. 'That, too,' he admitted. 'You have a real hellcat on your hands, Frank, even if she is one-armed at the moment.'

'I told you what happened, Leon. Nothing has changed. She and I made a deal, and we're sticking to it. I needed her help, and she needed mine. I had to know urgently what and who was behind the contract on my head, and she was in bits and injured. So we made the deal. We have helped each other.'

I shrugged and added, 'Soon she will be gone from here anyway, one way or another.'

'Let's hope so,' Leon said, 'for your sake.'

CHAPTER FIFTY-TWO

'A what?' Felix said.

'You heard. Lady wants a pardon from the president.'

Felix shook his head. 'She's deranged — and so are you!'

'It's the only way you're going to get the key that unlocks the encryption code.'

I was meeting him again, this time at a little car park on The Stray, halfway between Redcar and the neighbouring town of Marske by the Sea. We stood on low dunes overlooking the fine marine prospect. It was bitterly cold in the stiff breeze from the North Sea that was bringing foamy white breakers hurtling up the beach, making my eyes water. There was no shelter anywhere near, apart from the cars, and neither of us seemed prepared to sit in the other's car. It was going to be a short meeting.

'Do you, does she, have any idea what she's asking?'

'Of course we do,' I told him. 'She willingly cooperated with the CIA, and now she's able to offer you, and the president, the opportunity to make a major impact on a strategic threat to the United States. In return, she humbly requests the granting of a pardon for the things done that have put her in her terrible position. Surely that's not too much to ask?'

He gave a snort of derision, probably also of disbelief, and half turned away from me. I did my utmost to avoid smiling. I had him, and he knew it. He didn't know what to do. He wanted that password so badly that he could taste it.

'I need to meet Lady herself,' Felix snapped. 'We need to put an end to this nonsense. She needs to be reminded why she was brought out of prison.'

I shook my head. 'That's not going to happen. She has too much to lose. She's out of prison right now, and determined to stay that way.'

'How about alive? Does she want to stay alive, too?'

I stared hard at him. 'Don't even think about that as an option,' I warned him. 'If anything were to happen to her, the automatic disclosure of a package currently lodged with lawyers will go worldwide and bring the roof down on you.'

It was bluff, but a tough enough statement for him to know it was very plausible. The CIA could do many things, but it couldn't with impunity override the law. If it did, and that was known, the consequences would be serious.

Besides, I'd been thinking for a while that it would be good insurance for Lady to prepare such a package and place it with a legal guardian. It would be easy enough to do. We should get on and do it.

'Where is she?' he demanded.

'Somewhere safe.'

'With you?'

'I'm not at liberty to disclose her whereabouts,' I told him, falling back on the pompous language that can be so useful during the early, fencing stage of negotiations. 'All I will say is that she is safe, and protected.'

What does that mean?' he asked with a sneer.

I stood my ground, kept quiet, and declined to participate in debating games with him.

'And just how will she prevent the Miskovs exacting revenge for her killing of their favourite son? How does she propose to get out of that one?' he added.

'They are a threat,' I acknowledged, 'and they've been trying hard to eliminate her, but they've failed so far. With the encryption key, of course, you could bring down the Miskovs and do Lady Day, as well as yourself, a big favour. That would also help the United States identify and eliminate Russian secret agents operating in the country.'

Felix pondered this. What I had just said made no real difference to his thinking. He knew all that better than I did. It was the situation, and what to do about it, that he was pondering. With good reason. He had a lot to consider.

'Will she stay around?' he asked.

Afterwards, he meant.

'Not for long. For her, this tranquil corner of the world is a quagmire, a war zone, and she's right in the middle of it. She needs to find higher ground.'

'How about you? What's in it for you?'

I gave a wry smile and told him I was an innocent bystander. I was only involved at all because Chicago had come to my front door, intent on killing me, and I'd had to defend myself. Personally, I would be happy just to see Chicago go back home again. Beyond that, I wanted to see the Miskovs brought down, and Lady Day given the chance of a fresh start in life.

He looked at me as if he wanted to spit in my face, but all he said was, 'I'll be in touch.'

Then he turned and got back in his car. I watched him drive away. He wasn't a happy man, and I felt quietly satisfied about that. Men like him can't be allowed to have their own way all the time.

CHAPTER FIFTY-THREE

'How are you, Sasha? Really.'

'I'm OK, thanks. Life continues to be interesting, and I have found a good place to live.'

'Venezuela? I'm surprised to hear you say that. It's just about the last place in the world I expected you to go when you left here.'

'Perhaps that was why I went there,' she said with a grin.

'What are you doing there?' I asked. 'Or is that a question I shouldn't ask? Are you still under orders?'

She shrugged. 'Not in the sense you mean, Frank. Not formally. But I am involved politically. I am working with the revolution to bring about democracy there after the failed experiment with the Cuban socialist model.'

'So you have severed your connections with Russia?'

'Not at all. Only with Red Star. But not everybody in Russia, or even in the Kremlin, is opposed to more democratic forms of government.'

'You're talking about people like Leon, perhaps?'

She nodded. 'Leon is not alone.'

I didn't press her any further. I knew from old that she would only ever tell me what she wanted me to know. Either she had been born with spy genes or her training had been very thorough.

'Anyway, it's good to see you again, Sasha,' I said, changing the subject.

She smiled happily. 'Our reunion is good for me, too, Frank. There have been times, many times, when I have missed you in my life.'

She leaned forward then to kiss me on the cheek. I knew it was a token of her regard for me as a friend, not a hint that she wished to renew a more intimate relationship. I gave her an affectionate hug in response. She knew she was as welcome here as she had always been.

Leon called from the cottage to say he had to go.

I waved acknowledgement. Then I looked at Sasha questioningly.

'I will stay for a day or two,' she said, 'if that is OK with you?'

'Of course it is.'

* * *

We watched the chopper depart, taking only Leon with it. When it was a distant speck out over the sea, Sasha asked if Jimmy Mack's hut was still there.

'Still there,' I told her. 'Still in one piece. Jimmy made it to last.'

'I would like to visit the beach.'

'Go ahead. You know where it is. I'd better stay here, in case something happens.'

She set off. I walked back to the cottage.

Lady Day had been watching, I realized. 'How very romantic!' she said with a grin. 'Something going on between you two? For old times' sake?'

'Don't you start,' I warned her with a frown. 'I've got enough to think and worry about.'

* * *

I was a bit worried about Lady and Sasha being in close proximity. A pair of alpha females, proven killers both? How was that going to work out?

Sasha and I had been through some tough times together and had grown pretty close, intimate even, for a time. For a moment, I had even entertained the fanciful thought of Sasha living with me at Risky Point, once she came to the conclusion that her life as an intelligence agent was over.

That moment had been fleeting. Wiser counsel had prevailed. Sasha herself had pointed out that she would henceforth be a target for Red Star, and that neither of us would ever be, or feel, safe with them after us. Time is never called on Kremlin grudges, she had affirmed.

So she had left, insisting that it was in both our interests that I shouldn't know where she was going or have any way of contacting her in future. It had been a bittersweet moment, probably more for me than for her. Sasha had lived the life of a lone wolf in hostile territory for many years. Sentimentality wasn't in her make-up.

Now here she was, back again, several years later. I wondered if she would misjudge the situation and take exception to a woman she might think of as her replacement.

I also wondered if Lady might feel it necessary to be on her mettle and square up to a woman she had heard so much about, and who she had come here to find and perhaps kill.

One way or another, there seemed potential for sparks to fly.

* * *

My misgivings and fears seemed fully justified at first. Lady positively bristled when Leon departed, leaving Sasha at Risky Point, and Sasha made clear her disdain. But that was a phase that soon passed. It wasn't long before they were speaking in a civil way to one another, and over the next couple of days they began to have extended conversations. What they were talking about was a mystery to me at first. Guns, assassination tactics, fashion even — I had no idea.

Then I began to overhear snatches of conversation that reassured and intrigued me.

'Venezuela?' I heard Lady say. 'They've got a load of trouble there, haven't they?'

Sasha nodded. 'Much trouble at the moment, yes. But change is coming.'

'You think?'

'I do. There are forces in the country that won't accept the current situation for ever.'

'The army, you mean?'

Sasha shook her head. 'No, not the army, or the other military forces. They all do very well from the current regime. I mean other forces, forces growing from the people.'

'Revolution?'

'Exactly.'

I moved away, thinking how strange it was to hear the idea that revolution might be used to unseat a left-wing government. *How times have changed*, I thought. But not in the way Bob Dylan meant all those years ago.

I also wondered how exactly Sasha was involved in what was going on down there in South America. It wouldn't be like her to watch revolution happen and not be a part of it.

Goodness knew what Lady made of it. I was just happy that the bristling between them had stopped. There was enough to worry about without that.

CHAPTER FIFTY-FOUR

There were three of us now to keep watch, and we did. There was always one of us who wasn't asleep, resting or doing chores. Always one of us outside, keeping an eye on things.

There were also Leon's men, of course, but we never saw them after an initial meeting with Dmitri. They just disappeared into the background, doing their special-forces thing. The trouble with that was, it was the *foreground* where I expected something to happen.

And I did expect it. Something. Either Lucas would return, or Felix would decide enough was enough and call in CIA resources to mount an attack. Something, anyway. I had a very strong sense of impending doom in those few days when nothing actually happened.

Then it did.

* * *

It was my turn to be out and about, keeping an eye open for unwelcome visitors. I was halfway between the cottages and the main road when two Land Cruisers I recognized as Lucas's preferred transport turned on to the track. I grimaced and moved forward to meet them. I even had forlorn hopes of stopping them and making them think again.

Where the hell were Leon's men when I needed them? I couldn't help wondering, as Lucas's convoy pounded towards me, bucking and swaying on our gloriously potholed track.

Fortunately, the approaching vehicles did stop. Lucas got out of the first one, his injured hand and arm heavily strapped up.

'Out of the way, Doy!'

'Private land,' I told him. 'You're not welcome here. Leave before I call the police.'

He laughed at me. 'You're not going to do that,' he said scornfully. 'You'd have too much explaining to do. It's too late for that, anyway.'

He was right there. He knew it, and so did I. The time for calling in the cops was well past.

'Like I said before, we don't want you, Doy. Not now. We did at one time, but not now. It's her we want. The deal is she comes with us, and you stay right here. It's up to you whether you stay here alive or . . . or not. Now get out of the way!' he added.

'It's not going to happen,' I told him. 'Your best plan is to leave — now, while you have the chance!'

'Like that, is it?' he said easily.

I nodded.

As he swung himself back into the lead vehicle, I couldn't help wondering where the hell my backup was. Surely I wasn't as alone as it seemed?

Engines revved and vehicles moved. Briefly.

Even before I had dived out of the way, Lucas's vehicle bobbed and dipped and skewed round to the accompaniment of gunfire. I watched, astonished, as the tyres facing me shredded and chunks of composite rubber flew all around. Then the vehicle toppled and began to turn on to its side.

'OK?' Dmitri asked with amusement, as I got back to my feet. I spun round. He had appeared from nowhere.

I nodded, blew out my cheeks and said, 'You left it a bit late.'

He shrugged and grinned. Then he focused on the men spilling out of the stricken vehicle, herding them aside and forcing them at gunpoint to get down on the ground.

Lucas's men knew a sub-machine gun when they saw one, and had no objection when one of Dmitri's men started removing and collecting their weapons.

Meanwhile, the other Russians had surrounded the second Toyota with guns aimed and prevented its occupants spilling out to help Lucas.

Lucas himself seemed dazed and confused. A trickle of blood from his forehead suggested he had banged his head as the Toyota rolled, as well as having suffered a terrible shock and psychological blow.

The fight, such as it had been, was over. We herded Lucas and his crew into the remaining vehicle and urged them to depart. They seemed happy to have been given the chance and took off fast.

'You didn't want us to keep them?' Dmtri said.

I shook my head. 'Let them go. Leave it to the police to pick them up.'

'You're going to call them?'

'I must. I have a lot to sort out with the police.'

Dmitri nodded. Then he said, 'Job done!' with a big grin.

'Indeed!'

I smiled happily and shook hands with him and all his men, and thanked them profusely. Then we headed back to the cottage, where I managed to find enough bottles of beer for us all to have a modest celebration.

CHAPTER FIFTY-FIVE

Bill Peart wasn't too thrilled to get another call from me.

'What do you want this time?' he demanded.

'I want to help you — again! You didn't catch the Chicago mob, did you?'

'Not yet. They were not there when we visited. You were right, though,' he admitted. 'That address you gave me was where they had been based. So thanks for that. What I'm wondering, though, is how you knew. Care to tell me? Or do I need to come with a couple of colleagues and beat it out of you?'

I ignored all that. I wasn't in the mood.

'Well, here's another good tip for you, Bill. They've been here again, and have just left. About ten of them, all in just one of their Land Cruisers. The other one broke down while they were here.'

'How did . . . ?'

'Never mind all that now, Bill. They left a short time ago. I don't know which way they've gone. You may need the chopper to find them. What I would suggest, though, is that they're going home now. They'll be heading for an airport, but I don't know which one. If you . . .'

'I'm on it,' he said, and switched off.

* * *

It took an hour for the chopper to arrive to pick up my Russian defence team. I was fretting a bit by then, having visions of Bill Peart turning up while Leon's men were still here. I really didn't want to have to try to explain their presence. It would be hard to do that without digging an even deeper hole for myself. Russians on active service on British soil? The very idea of trying to explain it filled me with horror.

While we were waiting, Sasha confided that, if possible, she would like to stay another day or so, rather than leave with Dmitri and company.

'Delighted to have you,' I told her. 'Please stay. You might even want to visit Jimmy Mack while you're here. He'd be delighted, too.'

Or Jack Kerr, I might have suggested, a local fisherman based in Port Holland who had helped Sasha when she was last here.

'Oh, yes' she said, thinking about it.

I knew that it wasn't for me she wanted to stay. She had something or someone else in mind.

* * *

The chopper came in low and fast. One of Dmitri's men spotted it while it was still well out to sea, and the group were waiting with all their equipment when it landed. The pick-up was immediate. Within a couple of minutes, the chopper was airborne again and heading fast back out to sea.

'Impressive,' Lady remarked to me.

I nodded. *Well rehearsed*, I was thinking. Dmitri and crew were a formidable team, like the rest of the Podolsky staff. Leon ran a tight ship.

I was about to follow Lady and Sasha, who seemed to be heading for the beach, when the phone rang.

'Let's meet again, in the same place as last time — and hope it's a bit warmer today. I have some good news to tell you.'

Felix held my interest now, if not my confidence. Perhaps there really was some good news.

CHAPTER FIFTY-SIX

I went off for another meeting with Felix with Lady's blessing.

'Do what you have to do,' she said.

'I'm not taking the key with me,' I told her. 'I'll listen to what he says and then come back and talk it through with you. If we're satisfied, I'll phone him with the key. OK?'

She shrugged.

There probably wasn't a lot she could have said at that point, but I still had the impression that she wasn't all that interested. Her mind was elsewhere. Something else seemed to be engaging her. Nothing I could do about that. I would just have to get on and do what needed to be done.

* * *

Felix looked to be in a good mood when I arrived at the venue.

'Good news, Frank!' he said, giving me a charming smile.

'Tell me about it.'

I joined him on the grassy knoll from where he was surveying the scene.

'You like the sea?' I asked.

'Oh, yes! I have to admit, I prefer it a bit warmer than this one is likely to be, but I still like it. Most of my sailing has been on lakes, but when I retire, it's gonna be to someplace at the ocean's edge.'

'Live on a houseboat, maybe?'

'A yacht, more likely. I'm tired of flying over oceans. I wanna get down there and sail one!'

It was his call. I was in no hurry. I waited for him to quit fantasizing.

'The good news, Frank, is that it's been agreed — way over my head — to go for a presidential pardon for Lady Day. How does that grab you?'

'It's what we wanted.'

He stuck out his hand and I shook it. Seemingly, we had a deal.

'Any strings?' I asked.

'Nope.' He shook his head. 'Plain and simple, we'll go for the pardon.'

'With what prospect of success?'

He smiled. 'Come on, Frank! If I could answer a question like that, I wouldn't be working for a salary any more. I would be rich — and on board my yacht already!'

'Even so,' I said, refusing to be bulldozed aside, 'what's the likelihood of Lady getting a pardon? Best guess?'

He seemed flummoxed. 'This is the President of the United States of America we're talking about, Frank. Nobody second-guesses him.'

'Do I take your word for it that this will happen, or . . . ?'

'We'll hand it over to the lawyers. Yours and ours can sort out some sort of contract. Is that OK with you?'

I nodded. That seemed as good as it could get, frankly.

As nothing more seemed to be coming, I said, 'I'll run this past Lady Day. If she's happy with it, I'll phone you with the key.'

I think he was flabbergasted when I turned and walked away then. He had assumed I would be doing cartwheels in my delight with the news he had imparted. But I wasn't. I was a long, long way from doing that, because the pardon process had a long, long way to go before we could be sure about anything.

CHAPTER FIFTY-SEVEN

'The trouble is,' I said to Lady, 'that we have no guarantees — none at all. We'll just have to hope the commitment to seek a pardon can be legally sealed. I want to believe it will be possible, but at this stage there are no guarantees for you.'

'Doesn't matter now, Frank. Just do it. Give him the key.'

'Doesn't matter? How do you work that out?'

She shrugged.

'Even if Felix does what he says he'll do — or "they" will do — it still might come to nothing. As he said, no one knows what the President of the United States of America — this one, in particular — will think, or do.'

'I don't care anymore. Just get on with it. At least we'll bring the Miskovs down! That counts for a lot with me.'

'Yes, it will do that, all right. And I suppose we can always go public if nothing happens on the pardon front. Felix and his bosses wouldn't like that. So you want me to give him the key?'

'Yep. Just do it.'

So I did.

Felix said, 'You'll not regret this, Frank. Lady Day won't either.'

'God Bless America!' I said, trying hard not to sound sarcastic.

* * *

'You don't need to worry about me no more, Frank,' Lady said later, knowing I wasn't happy about things.

Worry about her? I smiled, thinking that would be a fine thing, if the day should ever come.

'No?'

'No.'

'Just remember, Lady, until the day the pardon comes through — assuming it does — your status won't change legally. The forces of law and order of the United States of America will see it as their solemn duty to continue pursuing you. Hopefully, minus Felix's help, of course.'

'It doesn't matter,' she said with a shrug. 'They won't find me. Even if they do, they won't be able to do anything about it. I'll be beyond their reach.'

'Oh?'

To me, it sounded like living hopefully. Not much security in that.

'I'm going with Sasha.'

'Oh? Where to?'

'Where she's going — Venezuela.'

She saw the look of sheer astonishment that must have crossed my face and gave me a crooked grin in return.

'It sounds like a lot of fun down there, Frank. I think I'm going to like it. I'm going to pitch in with her and help the revolution.'

'Using all your skills?'

'Exactly. Sasha says they've grown tired down there of trying to change the government democratically. In the next phase, they're going to pick up guns, and be real revolutionaries. Just like Fidel Castro did in Cuba in the nineteen-fifties.'

Oh boy! I couldn't help thinking. *The two of them together?* I wondered if Venezuela's president had any idea what was coming.

CHAPTER FIFTY-EIGHT

Lady and Sasha were off doing something together. I suspected they were down on the beach, having another look at the sea, which they both seemed to like doing. Maybe where they were going was a long way from the sea.

So I was alone, trying to get the windscreen wipers on the car working better, when I noticed a man walking along the track towards the cottages. I was sure I didn't know him, even though he was still a good way off. The way a person walks is a good identifier. We don't rely entirely on facial recognition, or even at all, when the other person is at a distance as this one was.

Not surprisingly, he stopped by the wrecked Land Cruiser and had a good look at it. I wondered what he made of it. It's not every day that you see something like that upside down on a rural track.

When he resumed walking, I set off to meet him. There was no point him coming all the way when he was at the wrong address. I could save him a hundred yards. Also, of course, this wasn't a time when I wanted strangers visiting me. Too much was going on that I would prefer to keep quiet and private.

'Can I help you?' I asked.

'Possibly. Are you Mr Frank Doy?'

I nodded.

He turned and looked back at the wrecked car. 'What happened?' he asked, as if he had a right to know.

'Accident. How can I help you?'

'Anybody hurt? I imagine they were. Hard to walk away from that without pain and scars.'

He was beginning to irritate me. I wanted him gone.

'Look,' I said, 'I don't know who you are. What is it you want here?'

'My name is Zimmerman,' he said, turning back towards me. 'I have come for Lady Day, and anyone who has been helping her.'

As he turned, I saw a gun appear in his right hand. The hand holding it was rising, and the gun was looking for me.

It happened so fast. My mouth opened as I prepared to speak. Then my muscles clenched as instinct and reflex kicked in and I prepared to hurl myself . . . somewhere, anywhere! I had no idea where. There wasn't time to think about it.

'Zimmerman!' a voice called.

He and the gun swung away from me, towards the figure rising like a wraith from a patch of reeds not ten yards away.

I barely had time to identify the wraith as Lady Day before gunfire erupted, two guns speaking at once, and Zimmerman reeled away before collapsing to the ground. Shocked, I could do no more than watch as his killer stepped quickly across and fired twice more, making sure that Zimmerman wouldn't get up again.

'You OK, Frank?' Lady Day asked solicitously.

I just nodded, confused and shocked.

She gazed anxiously at me.

My head began to clear a little. I became capable of thought and speech again.

'How the hell did . . . ? What did you . . . ?'

I gave up and shook my head. I needed to sit down. The world hitmen live in was too much for me.

‘We spotted him,’ she said. ‘Me and Sasha. I believed all along that he would turn up, and that it would be when people least expected him. That was how he always did things. So me and Sasha had a plan to watch for him, and deal with him.’

‘Well, you did that, all right! Thank you.’

‘My pleasure.’

I believed it probably was. My guess was that she had long wanted to go up against Zimmerman, if only to prove he wasn’t top dog any more. Left-handed, as well. Her right arm still in a sling. She had bested him good and proper!

* * *

We both looked round as Sasha approached at a jog, a big smile on her face.

‘That was so good!’ Sasha said.

‘Thanks,’ Lady told her.

‘Didn’t she do well?’ Sasha added, turning to me.

‘Just great.’

‘Now you can see why I want her with me in Venezuela. We’ll make a great team.’

‘I’m sure you will,’ I told her, turning away to walk back to the cottage. ‘I wouldn’t doubt it for a moment.’

My other thought was, *Watch out, Venezuela!*

CHAPTER FIFTY-NINE

Sasha said, 'You'd best call Leon, Frank. It's time for us to leave.'

Holiday over, if that was what it had ever been for her. Time for Sasha to see what Lady Day could bring to the table in her new workplace.

'Give us an hour,' Leon said when I phoned. 'Then we'll be with you.'

Sasha asked for the phone, as she wanted to have a word with him herself. She did that in their own language, which suited me fine. I wasn't surprised when I heard Zimmerman's name mentioned.

'He will do it,' Sasha said afterwards. 'Leon will take the body and dispose of it.'

By dropping it in the sea, presumably. I was happy with that. I would have enough explaining to do without another dead body being part of it.

* * *

Leon came with the chopper, again making me think he was based not too far away, whether at sea or on land. I told him that so much had been happening that I was going to have to tell the police some of it, if I wasn't to be accused of withholding information and obstructing them in the conduct of their duties. I was going to have to do it soon, too, as I expected them to arrive at any moment.

'In that case, Frank, we will leave now, before the police come, and let you do what you have to do.'

That made sense. The story would be a lot simpler to tell when Bill Peart arrived if there wasn't a helicopter standing at my door.

'I gather from Sasha that we will have an extra passenger?' Leon said. 'Two, actually. But only one alive.'

'That's right. Lady Day is the alive one. She's going with Sasha.'

'So I understand.'

'To Venezuela,' I added, with a dramatic shudder.

Leon grinned. 'I believe she might be happy down there. It will remind her of Chicago!'

We both enjoyed a chuckle about that.

'What about you, Leon? Do you have . . . business interests in that country?'

'Venezuela? Oh, yes. The world of business never stops, not even in wartime.'

'Russian interests there, as well, perhaps?'

He nodded. 'I walk a fine line, Frank. It is necessary.'

More like a high line, with a perilous drop on either side.

'But not with Red Star. I represent the good guys, Frank. Please remember that.'

'I know you do. You always have, Leon.'

'Come and see me again in Prague, Frank. I'm still based there, and I always have projects that might interest you if you're ever looking for work.'

'I might just do that, Leon. Thanks.'

Then again, I thought, my financial situation would have to be considerably worse than it was now before I considered that offer seriously. I could still recall with great clarity what working with Leon entailed. It wasn't for the faint-hearted. It would suit someone like Lady Day much more than it did me.

All the same . . . Leon always paid exceedingly well!

* * *

I phoned Bill Peart and gave him chapter and verse on the Land Cruiser occupants heading through his patch, while Leon supervised the loading of the helicopter. I thanked him for his timely help. Then we shook hands and he boarded the impatiently waiting chopper, which took off immediately. In a couple of minutes, it was no more than a speck in the distant sky. Gone. How relieved I felt!

'That it?'

'That's it, Jim,' I said, turning to see that well-worn, and welcomely familiar fisherman's face. 'Just you and me again now.'

'Not a bad thing, is it?'

'Indeed not.' I shook my head. 'I was getting tired of all the excitement.'

'Aye. Me an' all!' he said.

CHAPTER SIXTY

The landline phone rang. I frowned at the caller number I didn't recognize, but answered anyway.

'How are you doing, Frankie boy?'

I groaned. It was a voice I had hoped never to hear again.

'All right, Malky. What can I do for you?'

'Short and to the point, eh? Well, OK. Frank, I heard some people are looking for me?'

How the hell did Malkovich know that?

I shook my head and said, 'Not any more. They couldn't find you — and left. It was a false alarm anyway. It wasn't you they really wanted.'

'Good to know.'

'Yeah. For me, too.'

'See you, Frank!'

Not if I can help it, I thought, as I put the phone down. Even so, I did manage a little smile. Inevitably, what had started with Malkovich had ended with him. So nothing had changed.

* * *

Things didn't end there, not entirely. After everyone had left, I got to thinking that although it had been a pretty hectic few days, it hadn't solved any problems for me. I still needed to make some money. Also, I needed a change of scene and people. Risky Point had come to be a stressful place, not the haven it had always been for me. I needed to get away for a bit for a change, and to replenish the coffers.

There was always one place I knew I could go and be welcome.

So I phoned Leon.

'I thought I might be hearing from you,' he said with a chuckle. 'When are you coming to Prague?'

'When would suit you?' I countered.

'How does tomorrow sound?'

'Perfect!' I assured him.

THE END

ALSO BY DAN LATUS

FRANK DOY SERIES
Book 1: RISKY MISSION
Book 2: OUT OF THE NIGHT
Book 3: A DEATH AT SOUTH GARE
Book 4: LIVING DANGEROUSLY
Book 5: ONE DAMN THING AFTER ANOTHER
Book 6: SAVING HARRY
Book 7: BOROVKSY'S GOLD
Book 8: TERROR FROM THE SEA
Book 9: NOT DEAD YET
Book 10: THE HITMAN'S ASSASSIN

JAKE ORD THRILLERS
Book 1: NO PLACE TO HIDE
Book 2: NEVER LOOK BACK
Book 3: LAST RESORT

STANDALONES
RUN FOR HOME
AND THEN YOU'RE DEAD

Thank you for reading this book.

If you enjoyed it please leave feedback on Amazon or Goodreads, and if there is anything we missed or you have a question about, then please get in touch. We appreciate you choosing our book.

Founded in 2014 in Shoreditch, London, we at Joffe Books pride ourselves on our history of innovative publishing. We were thrilled to be shortlisted for Independent Publisher of the Year at the British Book Awards.

www.joffebooks.com

We're very grateful to eagle-eyed readers who take the time to contact us. Please send any errors you find to corrections@joffebooks.com. We'll get them fixed ASAP.

Printed in Great Britain
by Amazon

11770196R00123